DAWN AND THE DISAPPEARING DOGS

There, in the middle of the garden, was the stake with the chain that I'd clipped Cheryl to. But Cheryl was gone. There wasn't a Great Dane in sight.

"Oh, my lord!" I said. Pooh Bear and Jacques were still straining on their leads, but I pulled them back and knelt to look at the chain. The hook wasn't broken . . . My head was spinning. How had Cheryl run away? Had she worked the hook loose? . . .

Or had someone, for some reason, *let* her off the chain? Maybe some kid had come by and done it as a prank. I shook my head. There was no point in wondering about it. The main thing was that I had to find Cheryl. Soon.

Babysitters
MYSTERY

DAWN AND THE
DISAPPEARING DOGS

Ann M. Martin

Hippo

Scholastic Children's Books,
Scholastic Publications Ltd,
7-9 Pratt Street, London NW1 0AE, UK

Scholastic Inc.,
555 Broadway, New York, NY 10012-3999, USA

Scholastic Canada Ltd,
123 Newkirk Road, Richmond Hill,
Ontario, Canada L4C 3G5

Ashton Scholastic Pty Ltd,
P O Box 579, Gosford, New South Wales,
Australia

Ashton Scholastic Ltd,
Private Bag 92801, Penrose, Auckland,
New Zealand

First published in the US by Scholastic Inc., 1993
Published by Scholastic Children's Books, 1994

ISBN 0 590 55789 0

Typeset in Plantin by Contour Typesetters, Southall, London
Printed by Cox & Wyman Ltd, Reading, Berkshire

*The author gratefully acknowledges
Ellen Miles
for her help in
preparing this manuscript.*

1st CHAPTER

It's not that I hate animals. I don't. I think animals are wonderful. I like dogs. I like cats. I even like gerbils, although they are, you have to admit, quite useless.

But I'm not what you would call an animal *lover*. I don't have a pet of my own, and I've never really wanted one. I'm a vegetarian, but it's not because I feel sorry for the cow or anything. It's just because I don't really like the taste of red meat. And, while I understand that some people develop very deep relationships with their cats and dogs, I do *not* understand why they expect me to feel the same way they do about Fluffy or Fido.

Take my stepsister, Mary Anne. She'll hold up her kitten, Tigger, so that his nose is practically touching mine and say, "Kiss Tigger, Dawn. Tigger loves you." Yuck. I do not believe in kissing cats.

1

Or take Buddy and Suzi Barrett. They are two kids I babysit for sometimes. Buddy's eight and Suzi's five. They're both really cute: Buddy is quite skinny, with these big knobbly knees, and Suzi is a pudgy girl with pigtails and the most adorable little round tummy. They also have a two-year-old sister called Marnie. Anyway, I was babysitting for them on Tuesday, and we were playing with their bassett hound, Pow, and Buddy was actually encouraging Pow to jump up on me, muddy paws and all! I put a stop to *that* game pretty quickly, believe me.

Do I sound like a nut? I'm not. Really. I'm just a nice, normal thirteen-year-old girl. My name is Dawn Schafer, and I'm in the eighth grade at Stoneybrook Middle School. I live in Stoneybrook, Connecticut. I have long blonde hair and blue eyes, and I do all the things that nice, normal thirteen-year-old girls do. Except I don't kiss cats.

I'd been thinking about people and their animals ever since I saw Mrs Mancusi up by the elementary school. Who is Mrs Mancusi? She's a woman who lives not far from me. She and her husband have no children, but they *do* have about five million pets. Well, maybe I'm exaggerating. But they do have a lot of animals; at least one of every kind you can think of.

Anyway, on Tuesday I was on my way to the playground with Buddy and Suzi, and Marnie—and Pow, of course—and there was Mrs Mancusi, walking her three dogs. "Oh, Cheryl," I heard her say to the *huge* Great Dane by her side, "isn't it a beautiful day?" Then she turned to the little apricot-coloured poodle on her other side and said, "Pooh Bear, do you see the pretty leaves on that tree?" And then, as if that weren't enough, she called to Jacques, the golden retriever, "Jacques, you don't have to follow behind Pooh Bear! Here, go on and fetch the ball." Then she took this gloppy, disgusting ball out of his mouth (he must have been carrying it and slobbering over it all day) and threw it for him.

I just stood there, shaking my head. I mean, why talk to dogs? They can't talk back, can they? And there's no way those dogs would have understood a word Mrs Mancusi said. Well, maybe Jacques understood *one* word: "ball". But that's about it.

Mrs Mancusi waved to me. "Hi, Dawn," she called.

I waved back, but I didn't walk any closer to her because I didn't really have time to talk. (Not that she'd want to talk to *me*. But Pow was with me, and I thought she might want to have a long conversation with him.)

I was in a rush because I didn't want Suzi and Buddy to be late for softball practice. If they were late, Kristy would be annoyed with me; she just *hates* it when people aren't on time.

Who's Kristy?

Oh, boy, I'd better slow down and explain a few things. Remember how I said I babysit fairly often for the Barretts? Well, I do. That's because I love to babysit. And it just so happens that I'm good friends with six other girls who love to babysit, too. We're all part of a club: the Babysitters Club, or the BSC. I'll tell you more about it later. All you need to know for now is that Kristy Thomas is the chairman of our club. She runs all our meetings, and that's how I know about her hating people who are late for things.

Besides being our club chairman, Kristy also coaches a softball team called Kristy's Krushers. Cute name, right? The team is cute, too. It consists of about twenty kids, most of whom are too young, or not good enough to play Little League. Some of them are afraid of the ball, some of them can hardly lift a bat, and some of them tend to forget which base is first base. But they all have a good time playing, and Kristy is a great coach. And there are enough decent players on her team so that they even occasionally win a game.

"Okay, you lot, here we are," I said, when

the Barretts and I reached the playground next to Stoneybrook Elementary School. "I'm going to sit on the bench over there with Marnie while you go to your practice, okay?"

Buddy nodded and ran over to join the kids who were gathered around Kristy. But Suzi hesitated. "What about Pow?" she asked. "He'll be lonely without us."

"He'll be fine," I assured her. "Marnie and I will keep him company." I reached down and patted Pow's head.

"Well . . . okay," she said. She gave Pow a quick hug. "'Bye, Pow," she said. "Wish me luck! If I get a home run, I'll duplicate it to you."

I stifled a giggle. "I think you mean 'dedicate'," I said.

"Pow knew what I meant," said Suzi. She skipped off towards Kristy. When she reached her, she turned and waved. I waved back, even though I wasn't sure whether she was waving at me or at Pow. Kristy looked over then and saw me. She gave me a big grin and a wave. "Hi, Dawn," she yelled. "Hi, Marnie!" Then she turned her attention back to her team.

I watched the Krushers practise for a while. First Kristy gave them batting practice. She pitched five times to each kid (Kristy is always careful to be very fair), and gave them tips on things like how to keep

5

their swings level or how to step *into* the ball. Some of the really little kids, like Claire Pike, who's Suzi's age, needed special help.

"Claire," I heard Kristy say, "you've got to choke up on the bat."

"Choke the bat?" asked Claire. "Won't that hurt it?"

"Not 'choke'," said Kristy gently. "Choke *up*. We've been over this before, remember? It's when you put your hands higher up on the bat."

"Oh, right," said Claire. "Like this?" She moved her hands.

"Like that," said Kristy, smiling.

Kristy is *so* patient. I'm sure she's explained "choking up" to Claire about fifty times. But she never seems to mind going over things again, especially for the youngest members of her team.

After batting practice, Kristy went over catching skills. Then she arranged the kids in the outfield, and started hitting balls to them for fielding practice. The Krushers try so hard. They really want to do well, and they especially want to please Kristy.

During fielding practice, I saw Matt Braddock make the most amazing catch: he had to jump about three feet in the air just to reach the ball. Kristy gave him the thumbs-up sign instead of yelling out "all *right*!" the way she usually does. Matt grinned back at her. He's deaf, and signing is the only way he communicates. You would think that having a deaf kid on the team would be difficult, but Kristy makes it look easy. And the other kids love Matt—in fact, they've all learned a few basic signs, just so they can "talk" with him. Matt is one of the best all-round players on the team.

Soon after Matt's great catch, Kristy finished fielding practice and started to give some tips on base-running. Then she divided the kids into groups—each group included at least one older member—and gave them base-running drills. I noticed that Claire Pike's brother Nicky, who's eight, was one of the fastest runners. He also seemed to like sliding into base; by the end of the drills his white T-shirt was almost completely covered with reddish dirt. Luckily, his mum isn't the type to care too much about a filthy shirt. Nicky has *seven* brothers and sisters, and Mrs Pike stopped worrying about things like spots and stains a long time ago.

Once the drills were over, Kristy divided the kids into two teams and got a game started. "Pretend this is the real thing," I heard her say to them. "Pretend you're playing against the Bashers, and give it everything you've got!"

The Bashers are another Stoneybrook team. They are coached by a boy called Bart

Taylor, who is sort-of-kind-of-not-really-but-maybe Kristy's boyfriend. If you know what I mean. Anyway, the Bashers and the Krushers have a long history as rivals, and Kristy must have known that mentioning them would fire up her team.

"Yeah!" yelled the kids, as they streamed out on to the field. "Bash those Bashers!"

I watched the game for a while, and then I started to feel a little bored (sports were never one of my all-time favourite things and Marnie had fallen asleep in her buggy), so I walked over to the swings and sat down on one. Pow curled up near Marnie, and promptly went to sleep, too. I started to swing, gently at first. Then I pumped harder, and swung higher. Soon I was swooping through the air with my hair streaming behind me. It felt great! For a while, anyway. Then I began to feel dizzy. I think only little kids can stay on swings for hours. When you get older, that back-and-forth, back-and-forth motion can make you feel a little sick. I slowed down my swing and just sat for a while, staring around at the playground. It looked so familiar to me: the slide, the climbing frame, the picnic tables. But the funny thing is, I never went to Stoneybrook Elementary! I suppose it's just familiar to me because I've spent a lot of time at that playground in recent months.

I didn't go to Stoneybrook Elementary because when I was younger I lived in California. In fact, I lived there almost all my life. I only moved to Connecticut after my parents got divorced. When that happened, my mum decided she'd be happiest going back to the town where she'd grown up and where her parents still lived—and that town was Stoneybrook.

I missed California when we moved here, and I still do. I miss the warm weather, the more relaxed lifestyle, and most of all, the *beach*. But I've adjusted to Stoneybrook, mainly because I've made so many good friends here. My little brother Jeff never did adjust. He ended up going back to California to live with my dad. Mum and I miss him like mad.

At first I felt as if our family was shrinking. First it was the four of us, then it was just Mum and me and Jeff, and then it was just Mum and me. But my family started to grow again. How? Well, Mum met up with an old boyfriend of hers from high school days, fell in love with him again, and married him. (That's making a very long story very short!) And the best part was that the old boyfriend happened to be the widowed father of my best friend—now my stepsister—Mary Anne Spier.

I leaned my cheek against the cold steel chain that held up my swing. Just then, I felt a tap on my shoulder. "Hi, Dawn," said someone behind me.

I turned my head. "Mary Anne!" I said. "I was just thinking about you."

"Good things, I hope," she said. "Hey, listen," she went on. "I've just found the most brilliant new shop."

"What kind?" I asked. "Clothes? Records?"

She shook her head. "Nope," she answered. "It's a new pet shop, right in Stoneybrook. I was just there, looking at things for Tigger. It has a *great* selection of cat toys." Mary Anne sounded really excited.

Me? I'm sure my face fell. I'd been expecting something a little different. But I tried to hide my disappointment. After all, I'd hate to be thought of as Dawn, the Animal-Hater!

2nd CHAPTER

"So, be honest with me, Dawn," said Kristy. "How did the Krushers look? I mean, as a team?"

It was the day after my sitting job with the Barretts. It was a Wednesday, and it was almost time for a BSC meeting. Kristy and I were waiting for the other club members to arrive.

"Well, they looked okay," I said. "I mean, I don't know much about softball, but they seemed fine to me."

"I'm just hoping that they have what it takes to play against some kids from New Hope," Kristy said. New Hope is a little town not too far from Stoneybrook.

"New Hope?" asked Stacey, who had just come in. "What's going on there?"

"Oh, a boy who coaches a softball team there phoned Bart the other night. He wants to arrange a game with a Stoneybrook

11

team," said Kristy. "Bart and I haven't worked out the details yet, but it seems like it might be fun."

By then, most of the other members had drifted in. "Great idea," said Jessi.

"Let us know when it's set up," said Mallory. "It'd be fun to watch the Krushers play somewhere else."

Kristy nodded. "I will," she said. "Now, is everybody here?" She looked around the room. "Everybody but Mary—"

"Here I am!" said Mary Anne, bursting into the room. "Sorry," she said to Kristy. "I was playing with Tigger and I lost track of the time."

"That's okay," said Kristy. "You're not really late. It's just five-thirty now." She pointed to Claudia's digital clock.

I suppose Claudia's clock could be called the official timepiece of the BSC. It's fairly important to us. That's because we meet in her room every Monday, Wednesday, and Friday from five-thirty to six o'clock. During those times parents can call to book babysitters. That's how our club works. Simple, right? And parents seem to like it. We always have plenty of business.

It's a simple idea, as I said, but it's also a great one. Kristy was the one who worked it out. She's always coming up with terrific ideas. The BSC started before I moved to

Stoneybrook, but I became a member soon after I met and made friends with Mary Anne. The members are: me, Kristy Thomas (whom you've already met), Mary Anne Spier (ditto), Stacey McGill, Claudia Kishi, Mallory Pike, and Jessi Ramsey.

As I told you before, Kristy is the chairman. That's mainly because she invented the club, but partly also just because she's a good leader. Kristy likes to be in charge. I suppose you could even say she's a little bossy at times, but we're all used to that. Kristy's sort of a tomboy; she doesn't care much about clothes or make-up or anything. She's short for her age, and she has brown hair and brown eyes.

Like me, Kristy is a "divorced kid". Her father took off a long time ago, and Kristy's mum worked hard to bring up her kids alone. (Kristy has two older brothers and one younger one.) Those weren't easy times. But then something great happened. Mrs Thomas met a really nice man, started to date him, and ended up marrying him. Just the same as what happened to my mum. Only, in Kristy's case, her new stepfather really changed her life. That's because he (his name is Watson Brewer) is a real millionaire! Honest! Kristy moved to the other side of town to live in his mansion.

It's a lucky thing that Watson owns a mansion, because Kristy's family has really grown. First of all, Watson has two kids from his first marriage, a girl and a boy. They stay with their father every other weekend, plus two weeks in the summer. Second, Kristy's mum and Watson decided that they wanted to adopt a baby, so now two-and-a-half-year-old Emily Michelle lives with them, too. She's Vietnamese, and she's incredibly adorable. And finally, Kristy's grandmother Nannie moved in to help out. So now a *lot* of people are in and out of that mansion all the time. And since Kristy loves kids, she's in heaven with her large family.

The BSC's vice-chairman is Claudia Kishi. She's vice-chairman because—well, because we meet in her room. And we meet in her room because she's the only member who has her very own phone, with a private line. The club *needs* that line; we'd never get away with keeping our parents' phone lines busy!

Claudia is really different. She's absolutely beautiful, for one thing. She has *jet*-black hair, and almond-shaped brown eyes (she's Japanese-American, in case you couldn't tell by her name) and has the coolest, most unique sense of style I've ever seen. Claudia can wear anything and make it look like high fashion.

I think her sense of style is related to her incredible artistic talent. Claudia loves to draw and paint and make things like jewellery, and she's very, very good. Not just good for an eighth-grader, either. I mean *good*. Unfortunately, Claud is *not* that good at schoolwork. I don't know why, since she's obviously (to me) very bright. Sometimes I think it might be because she doesn't want to compete with her older sister Janine, who is a certifiable genius. Really. But maybe it's not that. Maybe it's just that she doesn't care much about school.

Two things Claud cares a lot about are Nancy Drew books and junk food. She's never happier than when she's reading one of those mysteries and munching on a Twix bar. But since her parents disapprove of both passions, Claud has to hide books and snacks all over her room. It's not unusual, when you're in Claudia's room, to lift up a pillow and find a Mars bar, or to come across *The Clue of the Black Keys* underneath a pile of art supplies.

Stacey McGill, our club's treasurer, is Claud's best friend. Like Claudia, Stacey is a great dresser. She's extremely sophisticated; she perms her blonde hair and really knows how to use make-up to bring out her blue eyes. To me, Stacey really looks the part of a New York girl, which is where she's from. She grew up there, and moved to Stoneybrook not long before I did. For a brief time, Stacey moved *back* to New York, when her father was transferred there, but then her parents got divorced and Stacey and her mum ended up returning here to stay.

The divorce wasn't easy for Stacey, which I can understand. I don't think it's easy for anyone. But she's adjusted to it. She visits her dad as often as she can, and she and her mum seem to get along really well.

Stacey's parents *used* to be very over-protective of her, because Stacey has diabetes. But by now Stacey has proved she knows how to take care of herself. She does, too. She gives herself injections every day (can you *imagine*?) of this stuff called insulin, which her body doesn't produce well enough. She's also *really* careful about what she eats: no sweets or junk food for Stacey!

Being treasurer is a fun job for Stacey. She loves maths, and she's great at it. Also, she loves to collect and save up our subs. We pay subs on Monday every week, and the money goes for club costs like Claudia's phone bill, or Kristy's transportation. (We pay Kristy's brother to drive her across to the other side of town to Claud's house three times a week.) It also covers supplies for our Kid-Kits, which are boxes full of toys and games that we bring along on rainy-day jobs. Kids love them. (Kristy thought them up, of course.) And sometimes we just blow some money on a pizza party for ourselves—if we can convince Stacey to break into the treasury, that is!

I've already told you a little bit about my stepsister—and best friend—Mary Anne. But there's still lots you don't know. For example, I'm not Mary Anne's *only* best friend. She and Kristy have been best friends since before they knew how to walk! Mary Anne and Kristy even look alike. Mary Anne has brown hair and brown eyes and she's pretty short. Mary Anne also happens to be the secretary of the club. She keeps the neatest, tidiest notes in our record book. She knows everybody's timetables, and she keeps track of all our clients. I don't know how the club would function without her.

I think Mary Anne is naturally neat and tidy. Maybe that comes from being the only child of a very neat and tidy father. Mary Anne is also very sensitive (she cries if she even *thinks* about something sad happening), a good listener (I suppose that goes along with being sensitive), and a true romantic. Mary Anne is the only member of the club with a steady boyfriend. His name is Logan Bruno, and he is very sweet.

By the way, you know how I said that Mary Anne and her father are very neat and tidy? Well, they really had a shock when Richard (that's Mary Anne's father) married my mum and they moved into our old farmhouse. Know why? Because my mother is *the* most disorganized, sloppy person on earth. Believe me, we've had to do a lot of adjusting and compromising to make our "new" family work. Neatness vs. sloppiness is not the only issue we differ on, either. For example, Mum and I eat only health food, and Mary Anne and her father love steaks. It's not easy, but we're all learning to live together.

You may be wondering what my BSC job is. Well, I'm what is known as the alternate officer. I can jump in and take over anyone's job, if I'm ever needed. For example, when Stacey moved back to New York for a while, I was treasurer. I like being the alternate officer. It's a special, different job, and since I like to think of myself as an individual, it's perfect for me. It suits my style. Besides, I'd hate to have to fuss with a notebook or an envelope full of money at every meeting. I just like to be with my friends.

Speaking of notebooks, I should tell you about one other thing we do in our club. We each spend some time every week writing up the jobs we've been on. We also read what everyone else has written. The club notebook is a chore to keep up with sometimes, but it's also very, very useful. It keeps us up to date on our clients—and on each other.

I think the only person who really, really *enjoys* writing in the club notebook is Mallory Pike. Mal wants to be a writer and illustrator of children's books, and she just loves to write. She even keeps a journal.

Mallory is one of our two junior officers. The other is Jessi Ramsey, who is Mal's best friend. Unlike the rest of us, who are all thirteen and in the eighth grade, Mal and Jessi are eleven and in the sixth grade. They are both great sitters, but neither of them is allowed to sit at night unless they are sitting for their own families. That's why we call them junior officers. They do a lot of afternoon sitting, which helps free the rest of us up for night-time jobs. That way, everybody gets plenty of work.

Mallory's probably such a good sitter because she's had a lot of practice with kids. She's the oldest in a family of eight. (Remember Nicky and Claire from the Krushers game? They're her brother and sister.) Mal has red hair and freckles and glasses and a brace, all of which she'd rather do without. She'd like to be grown-up and glamorous, but she knows she'll have to wait a while for that.

Jessi comes from a much smaller family. She has a younger sister and a baby brother, plus her aunt lives with the family. Jessi is beautiful, with soft brown skin, black hair, and enormous brown eyes. She's a really talented ballet dancer who is very serious about her art. She may actually be a professional ballerina one day!

There are two more members of our club, but they weren't at our meeting that Wednesday. In fact, Shannon and Logan only sometimes come to meetings, because they are associate members. They fill in whenever we're totally booked with jobs. They have really saved our skins a few times. Shannon Kilbourne is a girl from Kristy's new neighbourhood, and Logan Bruno is, as I mentioned before, Mary Anne's boyfriend.

So, that's the BSC. Our meetings are almost always fun, and the time usually flies by. That Wednesday was no exception. I was surprised when Kristy announced that it was time to adjourn. Then, just as we were getting ready to leave, the phone rang. I grabbed it. (Whoever's nearest usually answers, and I happened to be closest.) It was Mrs Mancusi. "I know it's short notice," she said, "but my husband and I just decided to take a little trip this weekend. We're desperate for a pet-sitter."

Guess who ended up with the job? That's right. Me. Not Kristy, who's mad about dogs. Not Jessi or Mallory, who are horse-

crazy and also adore *all* animals. Not even
Mary Anne, the cat-lover. Even though our
club is full of people who are wild about
animals, I was the only one available for the
coming weekend. But it was fine with me.
After all, work is work. And besides, as I've
said before, it's not as if I hate animals.

3rd CHAPTER

"I really wish I could have taken that job," said Jessi, after our meeting had ended and we were getting ready to leave. "I really like pet-sitting for the Mancusis. It's not necessarily *easy*, but it's fun. I love their guinea pigs, Lucy and Ricky."

"Remember that time you thought their hamster was sick?" asked Mal.

"I'll never forget it," said Jessi. "I was so worried about him. But then 'he' turned out to be a 'she', and she wasn't sick at all—she was pregnant."

"That's how we got Frodo," said Mal. Frodo is the Pikes' hamster. "And you lot got Misty." Misty is Frodo's sister, and she lives with the Ramseys.

Jessi smiled. "Yeah, that story had a happy ending. Anyway, Dawn," she said, turning to me, "when I pet-sat, the Mancusis gave me this information sheet about their animals. You know, what their names are, what kind of food they eat, how often they need to be walked, that kind of thing. It was really helpful, and—"

"And I have it right here," said Mary Anne triumphantly, pulling a sheet of paper out of the club record book. "I saved it, just in case we needed it again sometime."

"Well done, Mary Anne," said Kristy.

"You are *so* organized," I said. "Let's see that list."

At home that night, I studied the list carefully. There was a *lot* to learn about the Mancusis' pets! "Pooh Bear eats low-cal food," it said, "and it's important that Jacques gets a fish-oil capsule after his dinner." Further down, it said, "Don't be surprised if Frank talks a lot—he'll be lonely, and glad to see you."(Frank's a talking bird.) "Make sure Barney's cage is covered," the list went on.

I would *definitely* remember that. Once Mary Anne was visiting while Jessi was taking care of the pets, and Barney got out of his cage. This was not funny. You see, Barney's a snake. (They did find him and get him back into his cage, but it wasn't easy. Mary Anne *still* shudders whenever she hears the name Barney.)

I felt fairly prepared by the time I went

over to the Mancusis' on Friday night. They weren't planning to leave until Saturday morning, but Mrs Mancusi had asked me to come over a little earlier just to get acquainted with the animals.

I could hear the dogs barking as I walked up to the door—and there were some other sounds, too. Like meows and chirps and jungle screeches. I smiled to myself as I rang the doorbell. Dawn Schafer, Zookeeper. That's what I was going to be.

Mrs Mancusi opened the door. A big parrot was perched on her shoulder and she was holding a rabbit in her arms. She used her knee to push Cheryl, the Great Dane, out of the way of the door. "Hi, Dawn," she said. "Come on in! We're just giving the animals a chance to run around, since I'm sure you'll want to keep them in their cages over the weekend."

I nodded. Then I thought of something. "Is—is Barney out?" I asked.

Mrs Mancusi smiled. "No, he gets lost too easily. He's in his cage, safe and sound."

Good. Then *I* was safe and sound, too.

Mrs Mancusi left to put the bird and the rabbit back in their cages. When she returned, she introduced me to the dogs, even though I already knew which was which. She seemed to expect me to talk to them, so I said things like "Pleased to meet you, Pooh Bear," even though I felt kind of silly chatting with a dog. Then we walked through the rest of the house, and I met all the other animals.

"That must be Ling-Ling," I said, pointing to a Siamese cat. Ling-Ling yowled, loudly.

"That's right!" said Mrs Mancusi. "I believe you've done your homework." She seemed impressed. "And here are Rosie and Powder," she said, bending to pat two fluffy white cats.

"Powder is Rosie's mother, right?" I asked.

"Yes, she is. Let me see. Tom, the grey cat, is outside right now. He has a nasty temper, so watch out for him. And I'm not sure *where* Crosby is. He's an orange tom cat. He loves to play fetch, believe it or not."

Next stop was the study, where the bird cages are. I heard all kinds of chirps and twitters. "I used to have a bird, a long time ago," I told Mrs Mancusi. "A parakeet, I think he was. His name was Buzz, and once he flew into a bowl of mashed potatoes." Mrs Mancusi laughed.

Just then, from behind me, I heard someone say, "You got the right one bay-be—uh huh!"

"That must be Frank," I said. Jessi had

told me that Frank gets a lot of his lines from TV—especially adverts.

Mrs Mancusi nodded. "At first we tried to break his TV habit, but he loves to watch so much that we hate to deprive him."

After the birds, Mrs Mancusi showed me the fish, the rabbits, the guinea pigs (good old Lucy and Ricky), and the hamsters (none of which looked pregnant, fortunately). Then we went to the sun lounge. That's where the reptiles live. Mrs Mancusi seemed to love them just as much as the cats and dogs. She cooed over the turtles and whispered sweetly to Barney. "And here's our latest addition," said Mrs Mancusi, stopping in front of a big aquarium. "This is Petie."

I bent to look inside, expecting a new kind of turtle or maybe a frog. But what I saw made me give a little shriek and jump back. "What—what *is* that?" I asked. "A baby dragon?" In the aquarium was a huge lizard-like thing, with spines all down its back.

She laughed. "She does look like one, doesn't she? No, she's an iguana. Isn't she beautiful? She comes from Mexico, and she's the sweetest thing. Some iguanas will bite, but not Petie. You can pick her up, if you want."

You might think that touching Petie was the last thing I wanted to do. And I'll admit that I wasn't quite ready to go that far yet.

But you know what? There was something about that iguana that I really liked. I can't explain it. She was just as scaly as Barney, but she looked . . . friendlier. And even though she had those spines, I somehow knew right away that she was totally harmless. "Hi, Petie," I whispered into the tank. I smiled at her, and I could have sworn that she smiled back. Suddenly I was looking forward just a little bit more to my weekend as a zookeeper.

On Saturday afternoon, I went back to the Mancusis' and let myself in with the key Mrs Mancusi had given me. Cheryl, Pooh Bear, and Jacques practically *threw* themselves at me as soon as I opened the door. They seemed thrilled to see a human being, even if it was one they didn't know very well. "Okay, okay," I said, patting each one of them. "We'll go out in a few minutes."

I headed into the kitchen and found the new, revised list that the Mancusis had left for me. Using it as a guide, I walked through the house, checking on the animals and making sure each one had food and water. Then, just as I was about to check on the reptiles, I heard the doorbell. The dogs started barking so loudly I could hardly hear myself think. I ran back to the front door. I peeped through the spyhole, even though I was quite sure who it was, and then I opened the door.

"Hi, Jessi," I said. I'd talked to her the night before, and we'd arranged for her to stop by while I was checking the pets. Jessi lives very near the Mancusis, and since she loves animals, she didn't need much of an excuse to drop by.

"Hi," she said. "I brought Becca and Charlotte and Squirt with me. I hope that's okay."

"Fine with me," I said, bending down to poke Squirt in the tummy. Squirt is Jessi's baby brother, and he is so, so sweet. His real name is John Philip Ramsey, Jr, but everybody calls him Squirt. Becca is Jessi's sister. She's eight-and-a-half, and she's a bright, fun little kid. Charlotte Johanssen is also eight; she's Becca's best friend.

"I was just about to check the reptiles," I said. "You won't believe the new one they've got." I led everybody out to the sun lounge, and introduced them to Petie. Jessi thought she was pretty cool, but Charlotte and Becca weren't impressed. They only like soft, fluffy animals.

Cheryl had followed us to the sun lounge, and now she began to nuzzle my hand. "Oh, right," I said. "I suppose you're ready for your walk. Do you all want to come along?" I asked Jessi and the kids.

"Yes!" yelled Charlotte and Becca. "I'll walk Pooh Bear!" added Becca.

"I'll walk Jacques!" said Charlotte.

"Fine with me," I said, "but I'd better walk Cheryl. She's so big she could pull *both* of you down the pavement." We gathered up the leads, called the dogs, and headed out of the door. Jessi put Squirt in his buggy, and we started off down the street. The dogs were so happy to be out that they practically danced along the pavement. We probably looked like some sort of circus parade. I saw one car slowing down, as if its driver wanted to watch us go by.

We walked up and down the street a few times, and finally the dogs began to settle down enough so that I could relax and enjoy the beautiful day. Then I noticed something weird. That same car I'd seen when we first came out—it was an ordinary-looking dark green one—had passed us about three more times, going more slowly each time. We weren't *that* fascinating to watch, I thought. Or were we? Was somebody watching us for a reason? Were Becca and Charlotte in danger? I told Jessi what I'd noticed, and she and I decided that it would be best to go inside and give Charlotte and Becca our standard "don't-talk-to-strangers" speech.

"They've heard it before," said Jessi, "but you can't be too careful."

We took the dogs inside and settled them down. We talked to the girls, and then Jessi

29

took them (and Squirt) home. I double-checked the pets to make sure they were settled for the night, locked the door, and headed home myself. That car had given me a creepy feeling.

4th CHAPTER

I got up early on Sunday and hurried over to the Mancusis'. Normally I have a lie-in at weekends—I love to stay in bed as long as I can—but I knew those animals would be waiting for me. Not because they *liked* me especially, but just because I would be the one feeding them or cleaning their cages or walking them.

The dogs went crazy again when I let myself in. Cheryl jumped up and licked my nose. Pooh Bear darted off to get a toy, and then pranced around with it as if he were showing it off to me. Jacques ran to the kitchen, found his lead, and ran back to me, holding it in his mouth. "All right, you lot," I said. "Be patient. We'll go for a walk in just a minute."

At the word "walk", all three of them went totally mad. "Oops," I said, covering my mouth. "I mean, we'll go for a

W-A-L-K." This time, only Cheryl went crazy. "Oh, no!" I said. "You even know how to *spell* that word." I patted her on the head. "I'll just be a second," I said. "I want to check the other residents of the Mancusi Zoo."

I'd already become used to talking to the dogs. It didn't seem like such a strange thing to do any more, at least not when I was all alone with them. They couldn't *really* understand what I was saying, but they cocked their heads, looked right at me, and raised their eyebrows as if they were doing their best to make sense of everything I said.

I picked up my instruction sheet and started to work my way through the house. First, I checked in the laundry room and made sure the cats' food and water dishes were full. Ling-Ling ran to see me as soon as she heard the dry food spilling into her bowl, and right behind her came an orangey cat. "Crosby!" I said out loud. "How are you?" He hardly glanced at me; he was heading straight for the food. By the time I had finished filling up the water bowls, all five cats were chomping away.

I decided that I'd wait to feed the dogs until after I'd walked them, so my next stop was the hamsters and guinea pigs. Their cages were in the kitchen, and when I walked in, the first thing I heard was a funny whistling noise. "What is *that*?" I asked Cheryl, who was following along behind me. Of course she didn't answer. I shrugged. "Oh, well," I said. I checked the instruction sheet to see how much food to put out, and next to the guinea-pig notes I saw this: "Don't worry about that whistling noise. It's normal. Ricky does it more often than Lucy." Well, that explained *that*. I put out food for the hamsters and for Lucy and Ricky. Then I noticed that their cages could be cleaner. I turned around to find the sawdust, and almost ran over Cheryl. She looked up at me with her big brown eyes and gave a little whimper.

"What?" I asked. "Are you okay?"

She whined again and made a move towards the back door.

"Oh," I said. "You really need to go out, don't you?" She started dancing around as soon as she heard the word "out". I sighed. I wasn't ready to take the dogs for their walk. Then I remembered that Mrs Mancusi had told me about a chain-and-stake set up in the front garden. "Okay, girl," I said. "Come on. We'll clip you to that chain out there." Cheryl followed me to the front door, prancing and wagging her tail.

Before I opened the door, I grabbed her collar. I didn't want her running away on me. It wasn't easy to turn the doorknob and pull the door open and also hang on to a hundred and twenty pounds of dog. (That's how much Cheryl weighs. Mrs Mancusi told me.) Cheryl pulled me through the door, down the steps, and across the front garden. "No!" I cried, as we passed the stake with the chain attached. "Wait a second, you!" Cheryl let up a little when she heard me say no, and I was able to drag her back to the stake.

"Whew," I said, wiping my forehead after I'd clipped the chain to her collar. "You're a strong one, Cheryl!" She looked at me with her head cocked, and wagged her tail. "Okay," I said. "You stay here just for a few minutes, and I'll be out with Pooh Bear and Jacques as soon as I can. We'll take a nice, long—" I stopped myself before I said that "W" word. Then I patted Cheryl on the head and went back inside.

"Okay," I said, picking up my instruction sheet. "Now, where was I?" I ran my finger down the list. "Oh, right. I have to finish cleaning Lucy and Ricky's cage." To do that, I had to lift the guinea pigs out of their cage and put them on the kitchen floor. I felt a little nervous about doing that, but it worked out fine. They felt warm and soft, and neither of them seemed to mind being picked up. (I'd been worried that one of them might decide to bite me.)

After I'd finished with the guinea pigs

and hamsters, I went into the study to check on the birds. That room is *full* of big cages, and each one has some kind of interesting-looking bird in it. Mrs Mancusi had explained to me about the differences between macaws and cockatoos and the other kinds of parrots, but I couldn't remember which was which. The only bird that had made a real impression on me was Frank.

"Hi, Frank," I said, as I checked his food and water. "What's new?"

"New, improved Bounty!" he said. "The quicker-picker-upper."

I burst out laughing. "You are really too much, Frank," I said.

"Awk!" he said. "Energize it."

After I'd finished with the birds, I headed for the sun lounge. I checked on the turtles and the fish and then I fed Barney. Feeding Barney involves picking up insects and earthworms, which the Mancusis keep on hand. I try not to be squeamish about things like that, but to be honest it was pretty revolting. It was quite interesting though: I could see Barney's little snake tongue flick out, and then he'd open his mouth and gulp and the worm would be gone.

I turned to Petie, who was lying in a pool of light made by a lamp that hung over part of her tank. Mrs Mancusi had told me that iguanas love to be warm. "Hi, Petie," I said. "Remember me?" She barely glanced in my direction. I decided I'd been a little crazy to think she'd actually smiled at me. I fed her, and went on to the rabbits. Their names are Fluffer-Nut, Cindy, Toto, and Robert. All of them are white and fluffy and quite sweet, I suppose. If you like rabbits. I gave them some of their pellet food, and cleaned out their cages.

Then I checked my list again. I had taken care of everyone, so I decided to walk the dogs and then come back and double-check to make sure the other animals were set for the day. Mr and Mrs Mancusi would be home later that afternoon, and I wanted to make sure they'd be happy with the way I'd taken care of their pets.

"Pooh Bear! Jacques!" I called. I found the two of them in the living room, snoozing on the rug. They seemed a lot more patient than Cheryl. I found their leads, and as soon as they saw them, they went wild. "Okay," I said, stopping in the hall to attach their leads. "Let's go!" I opened the door, and they pulled me outside and down the steps, just like Cheryl had. They kept on going, too, just like she had, so at first I was too busy trying to stop them to notice that something was wrong. But as soon as I got them under control, there was no way to *avoid* noticing.

36

There, in the middle of the garden, was the stake with the chain that I'd clipped Cheryl to. But Cheryl was gone. There wasn't a Great Dane in sight.

"Oh, my lord!" I said. Pooh Bear and Jacques were still straining on their leads, but I pulled them back and knelt to look at the chain. The hook wasn't broken. I stood up again and let Pooh Bear and Jacques pull me out of the garden and down the pavement. My head was spinning. How had Cheryl managed to get away? Had she worked the hook loose? There's a dog that belongs to a family we sit for—the Perkinses—who can do that. Chewbecca is his name, and he's like Houdini. You can't lock him up.

Or had someone, for some reason, *let* her off the chain? Maybe some kid had come by and done it as a prank. I shook my head. There was no point in wondering about it. The main thing was that I had to find Cheryl. Soon.

I walked Jacques and Pooh Bear up and down the street, calling for Cheryl every other step. I also peered into every garden I went past, and watched for tracks. But there was no sign of Cheryl.

"Cheryl!" I called. "Here, Cheryl!" I was beginning to feel desperate. As a member of the BSC, I pride myself on being a *very* responsible sitter. How could I have *lost* one of my charges?

"Dawn," I heard someone call my name. I whirled around. Jessi had run up behind me. "I saw you go past our house," she said. "Were you calling for Cheryl?"

"Jessi! I am *so* glad to see you. Cheryl's missing! What am I going to do?"

"Missing?" repeated Jessi, her eyes round. "Oh, my—" then she stopped. She must have seen how upset I was. "Okay," she said, pulling herself together. "I'm sure there's no reason to panic. She can't have gone too far. I'm just on my way over to the Johanssens', to sit for Charlotte. She and I can help you look."

"Oh, thanks," I said, relieved.

"Why don't you go back to the Mancusis'?" she continued. "Maybe Cheryl has already gone home again. If not, you could use their phone to call Mary Anne. Then she can call some of the others, and we can start a search party."

I knew that almost everyone in the BSC had a sitting job that afternoon—after all, that was why I'd got the Mancusi job—and I realized that Jessi's idea was a good one. With all those club members and the kids they were sitting for, a lot of people would be searching. We'd be sure to find Cheryl in no time.

That's what I thought, anyway. But I was wrong. We spent the whole morning looking for Cheryl, and then I kept on looking right up until the Mancusis came home. Cheryl was still missing. It was really hard to tell that to Mr and Mrs Mancusi. In fact, it was one of the hardest things I've ever done. But they were nice about it. They said they didn't blame me, and that they were sure she would turn up soon. At least, Mr Mancusi said that. Mrs Mancusi didn't look so sure at all. She looked quite upset.

My weekend as a zookeeper had ended on a *very* bad note.

5th
CHAPTER

Tuesday

Claud, I think you were smart to stay with Adam, Byron, and Jordan today instead of taking the other kids to Krushers' practice. The triplets can be a real handful, but at least they don't throw temper tantrums in public.

Your right, Mal. Me and the triplets actually had a nice time together. They let me see their clubhouse and everything.

Wow! You should be flattered. I've never even seen their clubhouse.

Your not missing much. It's just a big cardboard box, like from a refrigerator or something. I don't even know how they all fit in their at the same time. Anyway, sorry you got stuck with Claire and her tantrum.

Since there are so many Pike kids, whenever Mallory's parents are going to be away they arrange for two sitters. Usually Mallory is one of them; she's been babysitting for her brothers and sisters for *ages*. And that Tuesday afternoon, Claudia was the other sitter.

"Claudia's here! Claudia's here!" Claire, the youngest of the Pikes, helped Mallory answer the door when Claud arrived. "Hi, Claudia-silly-billy-goo-goo!" she cried.

Claudia smiled and exchanged a look with Mallory. We're all used to Claire's "silly" mood. She's five, and five-year-olds can be like that. "Hi, Claire-silly-billy-goo-goo," she replied.

Claire giggled. "Come here," she said to Claudia, pulling at her sleeve. "I want to tell you a secret." Claudia bent down to listen. "You look pretty," Claire whispered into Claud's ear.

"Well, thank you," said Claudia, straightening up. She was still wearing her school clothes: a blue minidress with white polka dots, white leggings, and earrings that looked like big white polka dots. "You look pretty, too."

Claire was wearing jeans, a sweatshirt, and a wedding veil. "I'm a bride," she announced.

"I thought as much," said Claud. "Now, where's everybody else?"

41

"In the kitchen having after-school snacks. Come on!" Claire grabbed Claud's hand and pulled her down the hall and into the kitchen. Mallory followed them.

The kitchen looked like a disaster area. "Byron!" said Mallory. "What are you doing? I told you *not* to eat any of that cake. Mum's saving it for tonight."

"I *didn't* eat any cake," said Byron. He's one of the triplets—they're ten years old—and he knows how to put on an innocent look. "I just scraped away a little of the icing. You didn't say anything about that!"

Mallory sighed. "You're right, I didn't. So I'm saying it now. No cake, no icing. Got it?" She sounded cross, but she was smiling. She's used to the triplets' tricks.

"Got it," said Byron. "In that case, I'll just have peanut butter and jam, like Adam and Jordan."

"I'm not having peanut butter and jam," said Jordan. "I'm having peanut butter and ketchup."

Claud groaned. The Pike kids—especially the triplets—are always coming up with weird ideas about what might be good to eat. That's partly because Mr and Mrs Pike let them eat whatever they want, thinking there's no point in wasting time arguing about food with eight kids.

Nicky, who's eight, groaned too. "That's

42

yucky!" he said. "Peanut butter and ketchup. Ugh!"

"What are *you* eating?" asked Claud.

"Fig biscuits with Marshmallow Fluff," said Nicky proudly. "I made up the recipe myself. Want to try one?"

Claud shook her head. "Not today, thanks," she said. "I love each of those things separately, but together? I don't know."

"Smart move," said Mal. "Now, where's Margo?"

"She's looking for her Krushers T-shirt," said Claire. "Vanessa's helping her."

"Oh, boy," said Mal. "I'd better go and find them. Vanessa's probably already forgotten what they're looking for."

Margo is seven, and Vanessa is nine. Vanessa can be a little dreamy sometimes; she wants to be a poet when she grows up, and she walks around in a dream world. I think she's busy working out things like what rhymes with "rainbow".

While Mal was helping Vanessa help Margo, Claud kept an eye on the other Pike kids as they finished their snacks. Then, when Mal, Vanessa, and Margo came back, everybody pitched in to clean up the kitchen. The Pikes are used to working together, and they're a good team. Vanessa was assigned to wipe the surfaces, the triplets unloaded the dishwasher, and Nicky loaded it. Even Margo and Claire helped; Margo put away the ketchup, the peanut butter, and any other food that had been out on the table, and Claire swept the kitchen floor with her toy broom.

"Perfect!" said Mal, when they were finished. "You lot did a great job." She turned to Claudia. "It's almost time for Krushers' practice. Do you want to take the little kids over, or do you want to stay here with the triplets?" Margo, like Nicky and Claire, is a Krusher, and Vanessa is a Krusher cheerleader. The triplets aren't Krushers. They play Little League.

"Stay with us, Claudia!" said Adam. "We'll have fun."

"No, come with us," pleaded Margo. "I want you to watch me hit a home run."

"It must be nice to be so popular," said Mallory, raising an eyebrow. She looked around at her brothers and sisters. "I suppose none of you want your boring old sister hanging around, huh?" She pretended to be hurt.

"I want you *and* Claudia," said Claire.

"Thanks," said Mallory. "Now I feel better. But I don't think that will work out. The triplets want to stay at home and work on their aeroplane models. So we need to split up."

"I'll stay here," said Claudia. "I like helping with models."

44

"All *right*!" said Adam. He, Jordan, and Byron gave each other a three-way high five.

Mallory organized the other kids. "Now, does everyone have everything?" she asked, as they trooped out the door. "Baseball caps? Gloves? Trainers?"

"Check!" shouted Nicky. "Let's go!" He raced down the front path with Mal and the others following behind him.

By the time they reached the school, most of the other Krushers were there. I waved to Mal as she crossed the field. "Hi, Mal," I said. "I'm sitting for Matt and Haley." Matt's the boy I told you about before, and Haley is his sister. She's a cheerleader, too, just like Vanessa. Charlotte Johanssen is the third Krusher cheerleader, but she hadn't arrived yet.

Mal sat down next to me. "Has practice started yet?" she asked.

"Nope," I replied. "Kristy said she has a big announcement, but she's waiting until everybody's here."

Nicky, Margo, and Claire joined the other kids who were clustered around Kristy. Vanessa was standing with Haley, and the two of them were giggling. Mal looked across the field, and then back at me. "That's weird," she said. "I saw that car in the car park on our way over. I noticed it because there are hardly ever cars in it after school. Now it's sitting over there on the street." She pointed, and I followed her gaze.

I gasped. "That looks like the car Jessi and I saw the other day!" I said. "When we were walking the dogs. I wonder who the driver could be."

"Probably just somebody who likes to watch baseball," said Mal.

"Maybe," I said. "But it makes me nervous. I think we should bring this up at our meeting tomorrow. I mean, maybe we should go over the 'stranger' rules with *all* the kids we sit for."

Mal agreed. "Hey," she asked. "Speaking of walking dogs, have the Mancusis found Cheryl yet?"

I shook my head. "Nope. I can't believe it, but she's still missing. I've spent a lot of time looking for her, and so have the Mancusis. I feel terrible."

"She'll come back," said Mallory. "Remember that book *The Incredible Journey*? Those dogs found their way across the country to their masters."

"You're probably right," I said. "In fact, I could even imagine Cheryl's turning up here, today. Look at all these other dogs running around. They love this field."

Mallory looked around. "There's Shannon," she said, pointing to a big black, brown, and white puppy. Shannon belongs to David Michael, Kristy's younger brother. She is a Bernese mountain dog, and she's going to be gigantic when she grows up. She was playing with a smaller, brown dog. "And there's Bo, the Rodowskys' dog." Jackie Rodowsky is a Krusher.

"The Barretts brought Pow again," I added. "I hope he doesn't jump up on me today."

"Okay, everybody," shouted Kristy suddenly. Mallory and I turned to listen to her. "I think we're all here," she went on. "Now, before we get started, I have an announcement to make." She paused for a second. "Jackie, are you listening?"

Jackie put down the ball he'd been tossing. "Yup," he said, blushing.

"Okay," said Kristy. "Here's the announcement. Bart knows a boy who lives in New Hope and manages a softball team. He wants to play a game against a team from Stoneybrook!"

"Yeah!" yelled Nicky. "Let's go, Krushers!"

"Hold on," said Kristy. "Before you get too excited, I want to explain how we're going to do this. What Bart and I decided was that we should make a Stoneybrook All-Star team out of players from both the Krushers and the Bashers. Guess what the team will be called?"

"What?" asked several kids.

"The Krashers!" said Kristy, smiling. The kids laughed. "But the thing is," continued Kristy, looking more serious, "that only the older kids are going to be in this team. For a lot of reasons."

I knew, and Mallory probably knew, what those reasons were. Mainly, it was because the older kids were better players, and Kristy and Bart wanted to *win* that game. Kristy wasn't about to say so, though. She was trying not to hurt anyone's feelings.

It didn't work so well, though. I could see that some of the younger kids felt bad about not being on the team. Suzi Barrett had stuck her lip out about a mile, and Myriah Perkins, who's also five, looked like she was about to cry. But Claire was the one who really let her feelings be known.

First, she just frowned. Then she started to clench her fists.

"Uh-oh," said Mallory.

Claire stamped her feet.

"Here we go," said Mallory. "We're in for a real tantrum." Claire's softball blowups are famous. She doesn't have them as often as she used to—she used to get upset about every little thing—but once in a while she can still throw a wobbler of a tantrum.

Claire began to screech. "Not fair!" she yelled. "Not fair, not fair! Not fair, not fair, not fair!" The other little kids looked like they were about to join her. That's when Mallory ran to pick Claire up and carry her off the field.

She calmed Claire down quite quickly and sent her back to Kristy, who had started practice in the meantime. "I saw that coming," Mallory said to me with a grin. "I love my little sister, but those tantrums are something else!"

Claire threw three more tantrums that afternoon. Mallory handled each one like a pro, but I could see that her patience was wearing thin. By the end of the Krushers practice, Mal looked worn out, but Claire was still going strong. Where do little kids *get* all that energy?

6th CHAPTER

"Then she started pulling up handfuls of grass and throwing them in the air. That was when I decided it was time to go." We were waiting for our BSC meeting to start, and Mal was telling us about the tantrums Claire had had the day before. "Luckily, practice was just ending, so Kristy wasn't cross about all the Pikes having to leave."

Stacey shook her head. "Sounds like a rough afternoon, Mal," she said.

"It was," agreed Mal. "I'm just glad Claire only throws tantrums about softball. Imagine if she did that all the time!"

Claud stuck her hand underneath a pile of sweaters and came up with a bag of Kettle Chips. "Crisps, anyone?" she asked. She passed them to me, and I handed them right over to Mary Anne. I don't eat that kind of junk. I pulled out *my* snack—a bag full of wholewheat crackers—and offered some to Stacey. She smiled and took a few. The two of us share a special bond as the non-junk food eaters in the club. The only difference between us is that Stacey would *love* to eat junk food if she could, and I wouldn't touch the stuff if you paid me.

"So, where's Ms Chairman?" asked Claudia, after she'd watched her crisps do the rounds. "I mean, it's five twenty-five. I mean, oops, make that five twenty-six," she went on, after checking her digital clock.

"I don't know," said Mary Anne. "Kristy's usually the first one here. I wonder what's keeping her."

"She won't be late," said Stacey. "I know her. She'll pop in just before the clock clicks to five-thirty." She pulled a bottle of nail varnish out of her shoulder bag. "What do you lot think of this colour?" she asked. The polish was bright orange, with sparkles in it.

"Interesting," said Mary Anne.

"Sort of wild," said Mallory, sounding envious. "My mum would never let me wear that."

"I like it," said Claud. "Can I try some?"

Stacey tossed the bottle over. "Hey, look," she said. "It's almost five-thirty. Let's start a countdown, and watch Kristy burst in at the last second." She started to count. "Ten! Nine!"

The rest of us joined in. "Eight! Seven! Six!"

We were all watching the door, expecting Kristy to throw it open any moment.

"Three! Two! One!" we finished. The clock clicked to five-thirty. But Kristy still hadn't turned up.

"Wow!" said Mallory. "I was sure she'd get here in time."

"She's actually late!" said Claudia a moment later, when the clock had changed to 5.31.

"I can't believe it," said Stacey. "Charlie's car must have broken down."

"That's probably it," said Mary Anne, sounding relieved. "I mean, I'm sure there's nothing to worry about."

I could tell that Mary Anne *was* worried, though. She's the type who always imagines the worst. "She'll be here any minute," I said, to reassure Mary Anne. "And then we can tease her about being late."

It felt very strange to be gathered in Claud's room, watching the minutes tick by, without Kristy sitting in the director's chair.

"Do—do you think we should start the meeting without her?" asked Mary Anne, looking nervous. It was 5.36.

I gulped, realizing that as alternate

officer, I'd have to be the one to take over the chairman's job. I wasn't eager to jump into Kristy's shoes. "Let's just wait a couple more minutes," I said. We were all very quiet for a few seconds. I suppose everybody else was doing the same thing I was doing: listening for the sound of a car door slamming and then footsteps on the stairs. But no matter how hard we listened, we couldn't hear a thing.

Just then the phone rang, and we jumped a mile.

"Maybe that's her," said Mary Anne. "Answer it, answer it!"

Claudia grabbed the phone. "Hello?" she said. "Kristy?" She listened for a moment. Then she said, "Oh, sorry, Dr Johanssen. How can we help you? . . . A sitter for Charlotte next Monday? Sure, I'll call you right back."

Mary Anne looked crestfallen. "I was sure it was going to be Kristy," she said. She picked up the club record book to check on who was available. "It would have to be either Stacey or Jessi," she said. "But Jessi can't do it if it's a night job. Is it?"

"It is," said Claud. "So I reckon you've got the job, Stace. Okay?" Stacey nodded, and Claudia picked up the phone to call Dr Johanssen back.

"It feels weird to be going ahead with

business," said Mallory. "Without Kristy, I mean."

"I know," I said. "But we have to answer the phone if it rings, right?"

"Right," said Claudia, who had finished making her call. "Anyway, she'll be here soon. In fact—" she held up a finger. "I think I hear her right now."

Sure enough, Kristy burst into the room a moment later. "Sorry, you lot!" she said.

"Are you all right?" asked Mary Anne.

"What happened?" I asked. As soon as I saw Kristy's face, I knew that teasing her about being late was out of the question. She looked very upset.

Kristy sat down in the director's chair. "Just a second," she said. "I have to catch my breath."

The rest of us looked at each other, wide-eyed. "Kristy, what's *wrong*?" asked Stacey.

"Shannon's gone." Kristy stared down at her hands. "She disappeared this afternoon and we can't find her anywhere."

I thought of how I'd felt after Cheryl disappeared. "Oh, no!" I said. "David Michael must be going crazy."

"He is," said Kristy. "In fact, he and Sam are still out there looking. I only finished the search because I was late for our meeting."

"Did she run off?" asked Jessi.

"I suppose so," said Kristy. "We're not really sure *what* happened. David Michael was playing with her after school. They were out in the front garden. Then he remembered this ball he'd bought for her, and he tied her up for a second so he could go inside and get it."

"Tied her up?" I asked.

"On this run we have for her. You know, a wire that stretches across the front garden, with a chain attached? He clipped her to that."

"Then what happened?" asked Mal.

"When he came out five minutes later, she was gone," said Kristy. "The chain and the clip were still there, and they weren't broken. But there was no sign of Shannon. He ran in to get me, and we searched the whole neighbourhood."

"I can't believe Shannon would run away," said Mary Anne. "She loves David Michael."

"I know," said Kristy. "And he loves her. He's miserable, and he feels guilty for leaving her outside."

"That's silly," I said. But I knew just how he felt, because I felt the same way when Cheryl disappeared. In fact, I still felt incredibly guilty. "It's funny, isn't it?" I said. "That Cheryl and Shannon are both gone."

"Shannon's not gone," said Kristy. "She'll be back by the time I get home. I'm sure of it." She sounded firm, but I could see that she wasn't really so sure of herself.

"I've got an idea," said Mary Anne. She probably noticed, as I did, that Kristy was looking worried. "Let's make some posters. You know, saying that Cheryl and Shannon are lost. It will give us something productive to do."

"Shannon's *not* lost," muttered Kristy. "She's not." But then she looked over at Claud. "Do you have any cardboard?" she asked.

Claud started digging around for art supplies while the rest of us discussed the missing dogs.

"Maybe it's Alan Gray, or one of those other boys," said Stacey. She was talking about a bunch of boys in our class who are always doing obnoxious things. "Maybe they're just trying to tease us by letting the dogs off their chains."

"It had *better* not be them," said Kristy, sounding angry.

"I don't think it is," I said. "I mean, if it were just a prank, they would have brought Cheryl back to the Mancusis long ago."

"Maybe David Michael didn't clip Shannon's collar properly," said Claudia. "He's only seven, after all." She was handing out cardboard and Magic Markers as she spoke.

I saw Kristy glaring at her, and decided I'd better say something before an argument broke out. "I'm sure he did it properly," I said. "It's easy, and David Michael's a clever kid. Anyway, I know for sure that *I* did it right, and Cheryl still got away from *me*." Everybody was quiet for a moment after that.

"How does this look?" asked Mallory finally, holding up the sign she'd been working on.

"Great," said Mary Anne. "I love those sketches of Shannon and Cheryl."

We worked quietly during the rest of our meeting. The phone rang a few times, when clients called to arrange jobs. I know Kristy was hoping to hear good news from David Michael, but *that* call never came.

Not until I left the meeting did I realize I'd forgotten something. I hadn't brought up the issue of the green car, and we hadn't talked about discussing "stranger" rules with the kids we sit for. I reminded myself to bring it up first thing at our next meeting, on Friday.

7th CHAPTER

I forgot all about dogs, missing or not, when I returned home from our meeting that evening. "Mum!" I cried, when I opened the front door. "What's that I smell?"

My mother appeared in the kitchen doorway, holding a bowl. "It's your favourite," she said, smiling. "Tofu and vegetable curry. With brown rice on the side. Plus, I made some seaweed salad."

"Wow!" I said. "What's the occasion?"

"Does there have to be an occasion?" she asked. "I just felt like making you a treat."

"Well, thanks," I said, giving her a big hug.

Just then, Mary Anne ran in behind me. "What *is* that smell?" she asked. "Did the waste disposal break down?"

"Mary *Anne*!" I said. "That's dinner. Tofu curry! And Mum made it especially."

Mary Anne gulped. "Oh!" she said. "Well, I'm sure it will *taste* really good. I suppose I'm just not used to the way it smells."

Mum laughed and reached out to hug Mary Anne. "I'd never make my favourite stepdaughter eat anything she hated," she said. "Or my husband, for that matter. I made lasagne for you and Richard. It should be ready in a minute."

Mary Anne looked relieved. "Oh, that's great. Thanks, Sharon! And I'll at least try a bite of what you made for Dawn."

As I said, my new family is learning how to live together happily, but it still takes some work.

"I'm going up to change my clothes," I said. Although I never wear *anything* that's not completely comfortable (my friends call my style "California Casual"), I still like to get out of my school clothes and into jeans at the end of the day.

I headed up the narrow, creaky stairs. Our house, as I may have mentioned before, is really old. It was built in 1795, to be exact. And back in those days, people were smaller. Or at least shorter. Anyway, the ceilings in our house are very low, and the corridors are narrow. Other people might think it seems cramped, or strange—but I love it. This house has a lot of character. Not only that, it may have a ghost! That's right. There are some stories about a crazy man named Jared Mullray who may actually haunt this house. The idea is a little creepy, but *deliciously* creepy, if you know what I mean. I love ghost stories, and the scarier the better. My favourite book to read and re-read is called *Spirits, Spooks, and Ghostly Tales*.

When I reached my room, I changed quickly and put out my school books so I'd be ready to do my homework after dinner. I love my room; it's really cosy. For a while, after Richard and my mum first got married, Mary Anne and I tried to share this bedroom. That didn't work out very well, I suppose because we each needed our own space. Now Mary Anne has what used to be our guest room, and we're both happier.

I don't think Mary Anne ever really felt comfortable in my room, anyway, because of the secret passage. That's right, there's a real secret passage in this house, and one end of it is in my room! When you push this spot on the moulding, a panel swings open, and you can walk through the passage. It goes down a flight of stairs, and then *underground* until it comes up through a trapdoor in the barn behind our house. Guess why the passage was originally built?

Because this house was a stop on the Underground Railroad, which helped slaves work their way North to freedom. Isn't that cool?

Anyway, the reason Mary Anne doesn't like the passage is that she's afraid of ghosts, and there have been times when we thought that the ghost of Jared Mullray might be in there. We've heard moaning and scratching noises. The possibility of a ghost doesn't scare me at all—or at least, if it does scare me I don't mind—but Mary Anne becomes panicked at the idea of spirits anywhere near her.

I pushed the moulding to make the panel swing open for a minute. Sometimes I do that, even if I'm not planning to go into the passage. I just like to know it's there. I peered into the musty darkness. "Hellooo, Jared," I called. I giggled. What if I heard someone say, "Hellooo, Dawn!" in return? *That* might scare me. Luckily, I didn't hear a thing. I closed the panel and headed downstairs.

Richard had come home, so Mary Anne and I set the table quickly and my family sat down to dinner. I dug into the tofu curry, ignoring the lasagne that sat between Mary Anne and Richard. "This is great, Mum," I said. "You haven't made this for a long time."

"Glad you like it, dear," she said. "How's the lasagne?" she asked the others.

"Perfect," said Richard.

I noticed that Mary Anne ate two servings of lasagne before she even tried a tiny bite of the tofu. "Well," she said, after she'd chewed for a moment. "It's— different." Then she put down her fork. "I think I'm full. Thanks for making it, though, Sharon."

Good old sensitive Mary Anne. She always does her best to make people feel good.

"Richard, would you like to try some?" asked Mum.

He looked up from his lasagne, surprised. "Um, well," he said. "Actually, I'm pretty full myself. Couldn't eat another bite. It looks delicious, though." He blinked a few times and gave Mum a weak smile.

Mum laughed. "You don't lie very well, honey. But that's all right. I've learned by now that it's next to impossible to convert people to health foods if they don't *want* to be converted." She turned to me. "If you and Mary Anne will clear the table, I made something for dessert I think we'll *all* like."

She was right. The four of us gobbled down the blueberry-strawberry pie she'd made. I noticed that Richard and Mary Anne seemed to have room for *that*, but I didn't say anything. There's no point in stirring up trouble.

After dinner, Mary Anne went upstairs to

phone Logan. I settled down on the living room sofa. Since I didn't have much homework, I decided to relax for a few minutes and read the *Stoneybrook News*.

I glanced at the headlines and checked the weather. Then I started to flip through the paper. Something on the second page caught my eye.

DOG DISAPPEARANCES PLAGUE TOWNS, the headline read. "Wow!" I said. I drew in a long breath and began to read the article.

> *STONEYBROOK. The Stoneybrook police report a sudden increase in the number of missing dogs throughout the area. Dogs have disappeared from homes in Stoneybrook, New Hope, Lawrenceville, and other nearby towns.*
>
> *"Owners are reporting missing dogs at a rate I've never seen before," said Police Chief John Pierce. "The dogs have been disappearing from gardens and from public places, such as parks."*

The article went on to say that nobody had actually *seen* his or her dog disappear, and that the investigation had turned up very few clues for the police to follow up. In most cases, the dog had simply been unclipped from a lead or chain, and there was never any sign of a struggle.

I couldn't believe my eyes. This sounded just like what had happened to Cheryl—and to Shannon! My heart was pounding as I continued to read.

> *"Without any evidence to go on, we have no way of proving this,"* said Chief Pierce, *"but we do believe these dogs may have been stolen, perhaps by a ring of professional thieves. We will continue to search for clues and to pursue any evidence we turn up. Meanwhile, we are advising pet owners to be alert."*

"Stolen!" I said out loud. "Oh, my lord!" This was incredible. Was there really a dog-theft ring operating in Stoneybrook? I wondered whether the Mancusis had seen this article. I knew Mrs Mancusi would be upset to think that Cheryl had been stolen.

I thought back to the day she'd disappeared. Maybe I could come up with some clues. Maybe I could even help the police solve the case, and return Cheryl to the Mancusis.

I thought hard. I remembered letting myself in to the Mancusis' house. I remembered checking on all the animals, and I remembered the way Cheryl had followed me. After a while, I'd taken her outside and clipped her to her chain. Had I clipped her securely? I was sure I had. I thought about how I'd finished taking care of the other pets, and then had headed outside with

Pooh Bear and Jacques, only to find Cheryl missing. I'd checked the chain, and I'd looked around for signs of Cheryl. But she had disappeared. That was it. I hadn't thought of any new clues. The Case of the Missing Great Dane sounded just like all the other missing dog cases the police were dealing with.

I thought of how I'd walked all over the neighbourhood, calling for Cheryl. Then I remembered how Jessi had come out, and how we'd looked some more. I still wasn't getting anywhere. But then, thinking of Jessi, I remembered something. What about the day before, when Jessi and Squirt and Charlotte and Becca and I had walked the dogs? We must have been quite a sight. Such a sight that people driving by had slowed down to watch us.

Especially the people—or person—in that dark green car. The car! I smacked myself on the forehead. How could I have forgotten? That dark green car had made me nervous—*twice*. The first time was that day with Jessi, and the second time was when I was at the Krushers' practice, talking to Mal. I realized that maybe there was a very good reason it had made me nervous. Maybe it was because that car belonged to a thief!

I reached for the phone, thinking I would call the police and give them the important clue I'd come up with. Then I stopped myself. They'd be sure to ask for a number plate, and I didn't have that. Maybe I should do some investigating and look out for the car again instead. That way I could give *all* the information to the police, and they'd be able to crack the case in no time. Soon Cheryl would be back with the Mancusis, and I'd be able to stop feeling so guilty.

It was a great plan. I ran upstairs to tell Mary Anne about the article and about the green car. She was excited, too.

"Let's phone Kristy," she said. "I know she'll want to help. After all, she'd do anything to get Shannon back."

We spent the rest of the evening phoning the members of the BSC. (I completely forgot about my homework!) Everybody agreed to help look out for the car, and I went to sleep that night feeling sure that the case was as good as solved.

8th
CHAPTER

The next day was Thursday. My friends and I had agreed to meet after school and work out a plan for getting that registration number. By three o'clock, everyone was gathered at the elementary school playground.

"It was right over there," said Mal, pointing. She was telling the others about how she'd seen the green car. "Remember, Dawn?"

I nodded. "I certainly do," I said. "Boy, do I wish I'd noted that number plate right then."

"You couldn't have known it was important," said Kristy. "But we know now. And we'll find that car."

We decided to split up into pairs, just for safety. After all, the thieves could be dangerous. Besides, only a few of us had even seen the car before. This way, Mal,

Jessi and I could pair off with club members who hadn't seen it.

"I just came to hear about your plan," said Stacey. "I can't really search today, because I'm sitting for Charlotte Johanssen. But I'll keep my eyes peeled anyway." She headed off to her job, and the rest of us broke into pairs.

Later that day my friends and I gathered again to tell each other what we'd seen. I had asked everyone to take notes so we could submit a report to the police. (Everybody teased me for acting so official, but I was too excited about solving the case to care.) Here's what they wrote:

MaryAnne and I got on our bikes and started to ride around. First we rode by the Mancusis', since they have so many pets. Their home is like bait for a dog thief. But Mrs. Mancusi was out in the yard, playing with Pooh Bear and Jacques. So they're still safe. Then we rode over to the high school, to see if anyone was watching the people who walk their dogs there. —Mallory

We didn't see any green cars but we did see a lot of dogs. There was one little black one that could catch a Frisbee, no matter how far his owner threw it. —mary anne

68

After that, we just rode around slowly for a while, but we didn't see anything suspicious at all
— Mallory

First I showed Claudia a couple of cars that looked like the car we were watching for. Just so she'd know what color it was and stuff.
— Jessi

I'd call that color 'jade'.
— Claudia

Claudia wanted to stop at her house to pick up colored pencils to make a sketch, but I told her we didn't have time.
— Jessi

Instead, we rode our bikes over to the shoreline. I've seen lots of people walking their dog

69

there. The beach was really pretty,
and I sure wished I'd got my
pencils so I could draw it. —Claudia

I dragged Claud
away from the shore,
and we patrolled
the car-park. We
met a lot of dogs
and people, but
none of them seemed
like thieves. And
we didn't see any
dark green cars.
— Jessi

I liked that one big brown dog
that was chasing sticks. What was
his name again? — Claudia

Reggie. He was
cute. But we tried
not to get distracted.
We kept riding around,
looking for that car.
It was nowhere in
sight. —Jessi

Dawn and I decided to stick around the elementary school for a while, in case the car turned up. We sat on the swings and watched the people who came to walk their dogs. —Kristy

I just thought of something! I hope they didn't think we were watching them because we wanted to steal their dogs! —Dawn

I doubt it. Although, come to think of it, a few of them did give us funny looks. —Kristy

Anyway, no car showed up, so we rode around for a while. Down to the vet's office. Over to Carle Playground (we checked the Mancusis' house on the way). And past Brenner Field. We saw a few green cars — but we didn't see _that_ car anywhere. —Dawn

We rode for miles! But — no luck. I guess we'll have to try again tomorrow. —Kristy

As you can see, the afternoon was sort of a failure. But we agreed to try again on Friday, after school and before our club meeting. And that's when Kristy and I got lucky.

We had been riding around all afternoon. We'd checked the same places as the day before, and some new ones too. But we still hadn't seen any sign of the dark green car. It was almost five o'clock, and we were over on Reilly Lane, near the Rodowskys' house.

"Let's take one more trip past the elementary school," said Kristy. "Then we'd better quit and head over to Claud's for our meeting."

We rode for a while in silence. I was feeling sort of depressed. I had thought it would be so easy to find the car and help the police, but my plan wasn't working out the way I'd imagined. Then, just as I was at my lowest point, I saw something that made me slam on my brakes. "Kristy?" I said. "There it is!"

She screeched to a halt. "What? Where?"

"The car! Over there!" I pointed. A dark green car—*exactly* like the one I'd seen before—was parked in front of a house. Someone was sitting in the driver's seat. I could see the outline of a head and shoulders.

"What're they doing in this neighbour-hood?" Kristy wondered out loud.

"Probably watching somebody's dog," I said.

"I can't believe it. I'd like to go right up to that car and yell at whoever's sitting in it. How could they go around stealing people's dogs?"

"Kristy, don't!" I said, grabbing her sleeve. "They might be dangerous, remember?"

"I wasn't really going to," she said. "I just get so angry whenever I think of David Michael. He misses Shannon so much." She looked sad.

"Okay," I said. "Here's what we'll do. First, we'll park our bikes. Then you watch while I sneak up behind the car and copy down the number plate."

"Got it," said Kristy. I was surprised that she didn't seem to mind taking my orders. Usually she likes to be the one in charge.

We pulled our bikes over to the side of the road, and Kristy ducked down behind some bushes. "Okay," she said. "Go ahead. I'll be watching, and if I whistle, you come running back."

My heart was thumping as I sneaked up to the green car. I tried to stay low and walk near the bushes on the side of the road. Once I thought I heard Kristy whistle, and I nearly jumped out of my skin. But when I looked back she was waving me on. I crept

73

up until I was near the back of the car. (I didn't want to get *right* behind it—what if the driver suddenly put it into reverse?) Then I reached into my pocket and pulled out the little pad and pen I'd been carrying around. I'd been hoping for this moment, but now it was here I could hardly write because my hands were shaking.

Finally, I had written down the number plate. Then I ran, all bent over to look less conspicuous, back to Kristy.

After she'd given me the high five, we jumped on to our bikes and rode away as fast as we could. "Brill!" said Kristy as soon as we'd turned the corner.

"Thanks," I said. I was out of breath just from being so scared. "Do we have time to go to the police station before our meeting?"

She checked her watch. "Let's go," she said. "I think we can just make it."

We rode into town as fast as we could. The police station is a big building—the kind that makes *you* feel small as soon as you walk into it. But Kristy marched right up to the main counter.

"Yes?" asked a bored-looking police officer. He leaned over and raised his eyebrows. "Can I help you?"

"We'd like to report a crime," said Kristy. "I mean, not a crime exactly, but some criminals. Or at least one criminal."

"Go on," said the officer, now looking amused.

I broke in. "We have an important clue for you. It's about the dog-theft ring."

"Oh? Well, go on."

"We've got the number plate of a car that belongs to the criminals!" I said proudly. I was sure his mouth would drop open in surprise.

Instead, he yawned. "Have you, now?" he asked. "How do you know it's their car?"

"I just do," I said. "I'm sure of it. I saw the car driving around slowly, just before a dog I was taking care of got stolen."

"It's not a crime to drive slowly," said the policeman, smiling. He shuffled some papers on his desk. "Why don't you girls run along?"

I turned to Kristy. She looked angry. "Listen," she said. "This is important. What about all those people whose dogs are missing?"

"Right, right," said the policeman. "We're doing everything we can to solve the case." He looked at his watch. "In fact, I'm fairly busy right now . . ."

"Please," I said. "I've been working hard to get you some good clues. I can give you reports on everything my friends and I have been doing." I reached into my backpack.

He shook his head. "We don't need any more reports around here," he said, pointing to a huge stack of papers on his side of the counter. "But we certainly do thank you for your help." He looked at his watch again and picked up some files. "Now, if you'll excuse me—"

"Won't you at least take this number and check it out?" I asked. "I just *know* it's a good lead. Please, won't you?"

"Okay, okay, okay," he said. I suppose he was tired of hearing me beg. "Leave it with me, and I'll have someone check it out."

I had been hoping that he could punch the number into a computer while we waited, so I was quite disappointed. But at least he'd agreed to take it. "Here," I said, passing the paper over the counter. "And thanks. How long will it take?"

"Oh, a day or two," he said, yawning.

"Talk to you soon, then," I said, but I don't think he even heard me. He was answering the phone as we left. Kristy and I walked back outside. "Well, he doesn't seem to care at all!" I said. "Can you believe it?"

"I think he just didn't take us seriously," she said. "But at least he finally took the number." She checked her watch. "Wow! It's almost five-thirty."

We hopped on our bikes and rode to Claud's as fast as we could. We had a lot to report to the other members of the BSC.

9th CHAPTER

Saturday

Let's go, Krashers! I'm excited about our all-star game. I think Bart and I have put together a good group of players. The best of the Bashers plus the best of the Krushers equals "Look out New Hope All-Stars!"

I'm really glad that Bart agreed David Michael should be on the team. My brother is still broken up about Shannon, and he really needs some distracting. But I'm not so sure he'll be able to play his best until he finds that dog. His heart just isn't in the game.

That Saturday, Kristy was babysitting while her mum and stepfather were out at a lunch party. Kristy's grandmother had taken Emily Michelle shoe-shopping, and Karen and Andrew (Kristy's stepsister and stepbrother) were at their mother's, so Kristy had only one charge: her little brother David Michael.

It was the day after I'd noted the number plate of the green car. The other members of the BSC had been impressed by the detective work that Kristy and I had done. But by Saturday morning, Kristy had other things on her mind, and she'd practically forgotten about the green car. Saturday was the day of the first Krashers' practice, and Kristy and Bart would be coaching together for the first time.

Kristy was a little nervous. Since the Krushers and the Bashers were usually deadly rivals, it might be hard for some of the players to learn how to cooperate with each other. "I hope those Bashers behave," she said to David Michael as they walked towards the playground. "Remember how they used to tease us?"

"What?" asked David Michael, after a moment. He'd been peering into a neighbour's back garden as he and Kristy passed by. "Sorry, I didn't hear what you said."

"Never mind," said Kristy. She'd only

been thinking out loud, anyway, and there was no reason to pass her worries on to her little brother. He had enough on his mind. Shannon had been missing for a long time, and he looked for her everywhere he went, put out food for her every day (hoping to tempt her back if she had run away), and carried a lead with him at all times, just in case he found her.

Kristy gave David Michael a pat on the shoulder. "Hang in there," she said. "I'm sure we'll be seeing Shannon again soon." Actually, Kristy wasn't sure at all, but she felt she had to say something to cheer David Michael up. He looked so miserable.

"Remember when we first got Shannon?" David Michael asked. He took Kristy's hand for a moment, as if he were a much younger kid.

"I'll never forget it," she answered. "She was the cutest thing I'd ever seen. She made me feel happy again, even though I was sad about Louie."

Louie was a collie. He'd belonged to the Thomases, and Kristy and David Michael had loved him with all their hearts. Kristy even has a baseball cap with a picture of a collie on it; it's one of her favourite possessions.

But Louie, who was quite old, got very ill and had to be put to sleep. This happened soon after Kristy had moved into Watson's mansion. She was having a hard time fitting in to her new neighbourhood, and one of the reasons was that she thought the other kids who lived there were snobby. They all seemed to have beautiful pedigree pets, and some of them made fun of scruffy old Louie.

Soon after he died, though, one of those neighbours made peace—and made friends—with Kristy. The neighbour was Shannon Kilbourne (one of our associate members, remember?), and she made peace by giving David Michael a puppy. A Bernese mountain dog puppy, to be exact. And you can probably imagine how that puppy got her name. It was David Michael's idea to name her after Shannon Kilbourne. So now there are two Shannons in that neighbourhood: one human and one canine.

Or at least there *were* two.

"Shannon didn't replace Louie," mused David Michael, who was still gripping Kristy's hand. "Nobody could do that. But I really did—*do* love her."

"Me, too," said Kristy. She gave his hand a squeeze.

"Look!" said David Michael, pulling his hand away. "There's one of our posters." He ran to a sign posted on a telegraph pole. "I just want to check that the right phone number is on this," he said. "I mean, what if somebody found her but they couldn't tell us because the number was wrong?"

"Don't worry," said Kristy. "We were very careful to get everything right when we made those posters."

"Oh, yeah?" asked David Michael. "What about this?" He pointed to the heading on the sign. MISING DOG, it said. NAME: SHANNUN. BREED: BERNAISE MOUNTAIN DOG. "Aren't a lot of words spelled wrong in this poster?"

"Oops," said Kristy. "You're right. Claud must have made that one, and she's not the world's greatest speller. But look," she said, pointing, "the phone number is right. Even Claudia would be careful about that."

David Michael looked down at his trainers and kicked at a stone. "It doesn't matter, anyway," he said. "Shannon's gone, and we'll never see her again." He sounded as if he were about to cry.

Kristy bent down to hug him. "Don't talk that way," she said gently. She gave him a squeeze. "Come on, now. It's time to play baseball."

When Kristy reached the playground, she saw that Bart had beaten her there. He and several of the kids on his team were throwing a ball around. "Hey, Bart," Kristy called. She gave what she hoped was a nonchalant wave. She didn't want Bart to know that she was even a little nervous about their first practice together. She told David Michael to join the Bashers players. Then she headed for one of the benches near the backstop and started to look over her check-off lists of team members, equipment, and other details. Kristy can be very organized.

Bart loped over to where Kristy was sitting. "How ya doing?" he asked, smiling.

"I'm fine," said Kristy. "How are you?"

"I'm a little nervous, to tell you the truth," said Bart. "We've never tried combining the teams before. I hope it works out."

Kristy blinked. "You're nervous?" she asked. "Really? Me, too!" She heaved a sigh of relief. "I'm sure it'll be okay," she said. "Look, I've worked everything out." She showed him her lists. "All we have to decide on is the starting line-up, but we can work that out later."

Bart looked over what she'd done. "Hey, this looks great," he said. "You've got everything under control."

"Everything but the kids," said Kristy, pointing to the playing field.

David Michael was staring off into space as Buddy Barrett, who had just arrived, tried to get his attention. "Catch, David

Michael," said Buddy, throwing the ball. David Michael snapped to attention just in time to watch the ball sail by his head. It bounced to a stop in front of one of Bart's players, who was in the process of dropping the ball *he'd* just caught. Meanwhile, Matt and Haley Braddock, who had come with me (I was babysitting for them), were signing furiously in the middle of the field. They looked as if they were fighting about something, but Kristy couldn't work out what it was. And Jackie Rodowsky, whom we often call the "Walking Disaster" because of his ability to break things, make messes, and accidentally cause trouble, was busy distributing equipment. Bases, balls, and bats were strewn across the field. Jackie had picked up more than he could carry and was dropping things everywhere.

Kristy and Bart looked at each other, shrugged, and smiled.

"Jackie!" called Kristy. "Whoa, there. I think you need some help."

"Yo, Dave," called Bart, to the Basher who had dropped the ball. "Pick up the one behind you, too, and then bring it over here. Let's get organized."

Soon Bart and Kristy had rounded up all the kids on both teams, and everyone was gathered by the backstop. I sat on the sidelines with Mary Anne, who had just ridden her bike to the playground. She was out of breath, but she and I talked a little while Kristy and Bart did their best to organize the kids.

"I can't believe it," said Mary Anne, huffing and puffing. "I rode all the way to the town centre to do a special errand, and the shop was closed. Isn't that silly, to close a shop on Saturday?"

"What were you shopping for?" I asked.

"Oh, nothing," said Mary Anne. "Just a little something for Tigger." She glanced at me and blushed. She knows I think she's crazy to spend as much money as she does on that kitten. She's always buying him treats and special toys. Most of the toys just gather dust, too, because Tigger would rather play with a plastic straw than anything else!

"They had such great cat toys at that new pet shop," Mary Anne went on. "I was so disappointed when I saw that it was closed. I rode all the way there for nothing! I suppose I should have phoned first, but I didn't think of it. The shops are always open on Saturday."

"Oh, well," I said. "I imagine Tigger will just have to be deprived a little longer."

Mary Anne made a face at me, and then smiled. "So how's the combined practice going?" she asked. "I talked to Kristy last night, and she said she was nervous about it."

"It's going to be great," I said. "Look, Kristy and Bart asked the kids to introduce themselves." I pointed. "That's nice."

The kids were lined up in two rows, according to teams, and each kid in turn was telling his (or her) name and a little about himself (or herself).

"Jackie Rodowsky," said Jackie. "Short-stop. Or second base, depending."

"Jerry," said one of Bart's kids. "Third base."

"I'm Haley, and that's Matt," said Haley Braddock. "You've played with us before, so you know that Matt is deaf. But he always knows what's going on, because he watches so well. I'll teach you the signs we use during games. They're really easy."

"My name's Joey," said a tall boy on Bart's team. "And this is Chris," he said, pointing to a shy-looking boy. "I'm on first, and Chris plays outfield."

The introductions went on, until they were suddenly interrupted by a yell on the sidelines. "Unfair! Unfair! Krashers are unfair!" Kristy looked surprised, until she turned and saw who it was. Claire Pike was parading up and down the third-base line, carrying a sign. Suzi Barrett and Patsy Kuhn trailed behind her, also carrying signs. The signs said things like, "Let Us Play!" and "Krashers Are Mean!"

Kristy shook her head. She looked as if

she wanted to laugh, but she kept a straight face. "Claire," she called. "Come on, don't be cross. You're still a Krusher, and we need you to help out with our all-star game."

Claire stopped yelling. "What do you need me to help with?" she asked suspiciously.

"I want you to be my Junior Assistant Equipment Manager," said Kristy, making the title sound as impressive as possible.

"Okay!" said Claire, grinning and throwing down her sign. "Can Patsy and Suzi be the Assistant Junior Assistant Equipment Managers?"

Kristy shrugged and nodded. Claire and her friends sat down by the pile of bases and gloves that Jackie had abandoned. The team introductions went on, and then the practice finally began.

"Any word from the police after I left this morning?" asked Mary Anne.

I shook my head. "I was sure they'd call by now," I said. "There'll probably be a message waiting for me when I get home."

But you know what? I was wrong. Kristy called later that evening to find out if the police had called, and I had to say no. I think she was as disappointed as I was. "Now that the first Krashers' practice is out of the way, I'm not so nervous any more," she said. "I'll be able to concentrate on helping you crack this case. We have to find Shannon."

"And Cheryl," I added. "We have to find them both." I was glad to have Kristy's mind back on the mystery of the missing dogs.

10th CHAPTER

That night at dinner, my mum mentioned that she and Richard had seen Kristy's mum at the hardware shop that day.

"You went to the town centre?" I said. "But I thought—you were supposed to be at home all day!"

"I was home *most* of the day," Mum said. "Nobody told me I wasn't allowed to go out at all." She laughed. "Sorry, Warden," she joked.

"Mum!" I said. "I was expecting a really, really important phone call. And now I might have missed it."

"Well, I'm sorry," she said. "But being your answering service is not my main ambition and function in life." She was still acting very silly.

I pushed away my plate of vegetarian chilli and crossed my arms. I just *knew* the police had been trying to call me, and now

89

I'd missed their call. I wasn't about to phone *them*, either, not after that one officer had treated me like such a pest. Now I'd just have to wait even longer, and hope they called again. Mary Anne gave me a sympathetic look from across the table.

"Really, honey," said Mum. "I'm sorry." She sounded serious now. "I didn't know. Anyway, whoever it is, I'm sure he'll call back."

She must have thought I was waiting to hear from a boy or something. I didn't want to explain what I was really up to, since Mum and Richard might think tracking down criminals was too dangerous for me. "You're right," I said. "It's okay. I should have told you I was waiting to hear from someone." I picked up my plate. "May I be excused?" I asked.

Mary Anne followed me upstairs and we spent some time talking over the situation, but without any new information from the police, there wasn't much to say. We ended up playing with Tigger, teasing him with a feather and watching him leap up and try to catch it.

The next day I did not leave the house once, not even to go out to the front porch and pick up the Sunday papers. (Mary Anne did that.) I also tried to make sure everybody stayed off the phone, since I didn't want the police to get an engaged tone when they called. I even cut short a conversation with my own little brother. Jeff phones once in a while from California, and usually I'm thrilled to hear from him. But that day I told him I couldn't talk.

I was positive that the police would phone me, but guess what? They didn't. I was quite disappointed by the end of the day, but I'd also made a decision. After school on Monday, I would go to the police station and ask them what they'd found out. If they treated me like a pest, I would just have to live with it. Mary Anne agreed to go with me, for moral support, and so did Kristy.

We rode our bikes into the town centre the next day, and walked into the police station at a little after three o'clock. It was fairly quiet in there; I suppose not much crime takes place on Monday afternoons. The officer at the desk, who was leafing through a magazine, was the same one I'd talked to on Friday. But he didn't seem to remember me until I reminded him of who I was.

"Oh, right," he said. "The girl who takes down details of number plates." He turned another page in his magazine.

"Did you check on that one I gave you?" I asked, trying to ignore his attitude.

"As a matter of fact, I did," he said. "And I hate to tell you this, but you're barking up the wrong tree." He paused, as if checking to see whether we'd got his little joke.

I gave him a tiny smile. I didn't think he was being funny at all. "Who owns the car?" I asked.

"Karl Tate," said the officer, a smug smile on his face.

Kristy and Mary Anne gasped, but the name didn't mean anything to me. "Who's Karl Tate?" I asked.

"Just one of the wealthiest men in Stoneybrook," said the officer.

"He owns property all over town," added Kristy. "I've heard Watson talk about him. He's an important businessman."

"That's right," said the officer. "Now, do you think someone like Mr Tate would waste his time driving around stealing dogs?"

"I suppose not," I said, feeling defeated.

"Don't get me wrong," said the officer. "This case is a priority with us. But we've got our own investigation going. A professional investigation. You girls would be better off spending your time on your homework, don't you think?" He picked up his magazine.

We left the police station. Outside on the

pavement, Kristy and Mary Anne tried to cheer me up.

"I suppose it was just a false lead," said Kristy.

"Yeah," I said. "A red herring." I'd picked up that term from one of Claudia's Nancy Drew books.

"Too bad," said Mary Anne. "But the officer is right. Mr Tate would never steal dogs. He loves animals. I've seen him down at that new pet shop." She smiled at me, hoping I would smile back. "Hey, I know," she said. "Speaking of the new pet shop, why don't we stop off there now? As long as we're in town, I mean."

"Fine with me," said Kristy. "I'll buy a new toy for Shannon. That will show David Michael that I really believe she's coming back."

"Great," said Mary Anne. "I still want to get that toy for Tigger. I just hope they're open this time."

I couldn't have been less interested in a trip to the pet shop, but I followed along anyway. Since the policeman had pretty much "dismissed me from the case", I had nothing else to do anyway.

It was just a short ride to the shop, which was open, so we parked our bikes and headed inside. Kristy stopped short near the front door. "Aww," she said. "Would you look at that?" She pointed into a cage.

Two black puppies and one white one were sleeping in a pile.

"Oh, aren't they darling?" said Mary Anne. She poked her finger through the cage to touch the white puppy.

"Mary Anne!" I hissed. "Be careful. He might bite you!"

Mary Anne just kept poking. "Oh, snoogums would never bite anyone," she said. "Would you, little bunky-boo?" The puppy yawned, and his pink mouth opened up wide. I saw a row of tiny, sharp white teeth.

"Watch out!" I said, just as the teeth clamped shut on Mary Anne's finger.

She laughed. "It doesn't hurt," she said. "He's just a puppy. They all like to bite and chew."

"Shannon used to do that," said Kristy in a sad voice. "She'd nip us all over, and then lick us as if she wanted to make us feel better." She had stuck her fingers in the cage now, too.

"You lot," I said, trying to be patient, "I thought we came here for a reason." I wasn't interested in hanging around talking baby talk to puppies all day.

"We did," said Mary Anne. "But I like to look at the animals when I come here. That's half the fun."

"Wow," said Kristy, pointing at a tank. "Isn't that the coolest fish you ever saw?" It was a big black-and-white striped fish, swimming to and fro with a mean expression on its face.

"Great," agreed Mary Anne. "And I love the way that tank is set up, with that pretend shipwreck and everything."

"I'd like to have a big tropical fish tank someday," said Kristy. "Like the one the Mancusis have. I love to watch all the fish swim around."

Personally, I thought fish were boring. "How about those kittens?" I said, hoping to distract Kristy and Mary Anne and keep them moving along. They got stuck in front of every cage they passed.

"Hey!" said Mary Anne. "Those are Maine coon cats."

"Coon cats?" I asked. "What do you mean? Are they crossed with racoons or something?" I giggled, but Mary Anne looked serious.

"That's what some people say," she said. "See how big they are, even for young kittens? And they have those stripes on their tails. I always wanted one of those."

"They're beautiful," said Kristy. "Maine coon cats, huh? I'll have to remember that."

I shudder to think of what will happen when Mary Anne and Kristy grow up and can have all the pets they want. Their houses will be like the Mancusis', only more so! "So, Mary Anne," I said, trying once again to move her and Kristy along. "Where are the cat toys?"

"They're at the back of the shop," she said. "The shops always put the cat stuff at the back. And they never have as many things for cats as they do for dogs. I suppose cats just aren't as popular. Isn't that unfair?" She frowned.

"It's terrible," I agreed, "but I thought you said you'd found some good things here."

"I have," she agreed. "Just wait till I show you." She started to walk towards the back of the shop, and Kristy and I followed behind. "Look!" said Mary Anne, when we came to the cat things. "Isn't this a great scratching post?" She knelt down to look at it.

Kristy and I stood there waiting while Mary Anne checked out some toys. "Hey, look," whispered Kristy to me suddenly, pointing behind me. "There's Mr Tate!"

I turned around and saw a man standing in the windowed office in the back corner of the shop. He was gesturing angrily as he spoke to a couple who were with him.

Mary Anne straightened up to look. "You're right, that's him," she said. "And the man and the woman are the people who own the shop, I think," she went on.

We watched for a minute. The three of them seemed to be arguing about something, but we couldn't hear what they were saying. Suddenly Mr Tate glanced over and saw us staring at him. He yanked down the venetian blind.

I looked at Kristy and Mary Anne. "Something fishy is going on," I said. "I mean, pardon the pun, but don't you think so, too?"

They looked back with round eyes. I could tell they agreed with me. Somehow we just knew that Mr Tate *did* have something to do with those disappearing dogs, no matter what the police said.

11th CHAPTER

At our BSC meeting that afternoon, Kristy and Mary Anne and I told the others about our day.

"I think that policeman sounds rude," said Mallory.

"So do I," said Claud. "But I think he's probably just overworked or something."

"Not only that," said Stacey, "but who's going to believe a bunch of kids?"

"But they *should* believe us," I said. "This is so frustrating. I just *know* that Mr Tate is involved in stealing those dogs. But I don't know how to prove it. And I suppose they won't believe us until we *do* prove it."

"I still can't work it out," said Kristy. "I mean, I had the same feeling as Dawn about Mr Tate. But why? Why would a rich man like that bother stealing dogs? It would be as if Watson suddenly started shoplifting or something."

"Maybe you've got something there!" said Jessi, excited. "Maybe it's like a sickness. Maybe Mr Tate is *driven* to steal dogs, for some deep psychological reason."

I looked over at her and raised my eyebrows. "That's a little far-fetched, don't you think? I mean, what kind of psychological reason could there be to steal dogs? For example, that he never had one as a child? But he could buy a million dogs if he wanted to. He's rich!"

Jessi giggled. "I suppose you're right. It is a little far-fetched. But how else can we explain it?"

"We don't have to explain it," said Stacey suddenly. "We just have to prove it."

"You're right!" I said. "That's exactly it. So how do we prove it?"

After a lot of discussion, we decided to break up into teams again, and spend Tuesday and Wednesday afternoon doing "surveillance". (Claudia's term. Again, from Nancy Drew.) We would stake out the pet shop, check on Mr Tate's home, and try to follow him when he was on foot. We'd also watch for the green car.

"Are you sure this isn't dangerous?" asked Mary Anne. "Or illegal?"

"Are you joking?" asked Kristy. "First of all, we'll be safe as long as we're in pairs. And second, there's nothing illegal about *looking* at someone. It's not like we're going to use force on him or anything."

I giggled at the thought of Kristy in a scuffle with Mr Tate. He was a tall, broad man with lots of thick blond hair. He looked strong and healthy—like one of those wrestlers on Saturday TV. There was no way any of us was about to mess with him. "We're just looking for evidence," I said. "Concrete evidence that the police can't ignore. And as soon as we have that, we'll turn the case over to them and let them take it from there."

The next day, as soon as school was over, we put our plan into action. We teamed up a little differently this time: Jessi and Mal, Kristy and Stacey, and me and Mary Anne. Claudia had a sitting job, but she promised to watch for suspicious characters in green cars.

Even though the policeman had turned up his nose at my reports, I decided to ask my friends to keep writing them up. They still might come in handy later on, I decided. So here are the reports for Tuesday's work:

Mal and I headed over to the Tates' house. It's sort of in Kristy's neighbourhood. We found

the address by
looking in the
phone book. —Jessi

Kristy, if you think your house is a
mansion, you should see this one. It's got
pillars across the front porch, and a huge
fountain in the front yard. It looks like
the plantation houses in Gone with the Wind.
— Mallory

We staked out the
house for two hours.
Here's what we saw:
Mrs. Tate drove in
and out twice (in
her red Mercedes).
We think she went
downtown the first
time, because she
had shopping bags

when she came
back. But we had
no idea where she
went the second time.
— Jessi

I think it was to the hairdresser,
because she was wearing this weird
scarf when she came back like she
was trying to keep her hairdo from
getting messed up.
— Mallory

Anyway, we didn't
see any familiar-
looking dogs, or any
green sedans. I
guess the afternoon
was a waste of
time. Except for the
fact that we got
to see how the
rich and famous live.
— Jessi

Stacey and I hung around the
playground for a while, watching
for the green car. We ran into

Mrs. Mancusi, who told us that Cheryl is still missing and the police don't seem to have any clues at all. She looked pretty upset.   —Kristy

Kristy wanted to tell her what we were up to—I know she did. But I kicked her before she could say a word. It's better if nobody knows.   —Stacey

My shin is still sore, too. But I guess Stacey was right. Anyway, we left the playground and went to the _other_ pet shop in town, just to check and make sure no funny business was going on there.   —Kristy

It seemed like a normal pet shop. So that was that.   —Stacey

We hid across the street from the new pet shop and watched for hours. At first nothing happened. People went in, people came out. One lady bought a Maine coon kitten.   —Mary Anne

That's when MaryAnne almost blew our cover. She wanted to run across the street and pet it. I had to hold her back. — Dawn

It's a good thing she did, too. Because right after that, we saw the green car pull out into traffic from behind the shop! — MaryAnne

We even got a look at the driver. And it wasn't Mr. Tate. — Dawn

It was the owner of the shop. I'm almost positive. — MaryAnne

So really, we're back to square one. — Dawn

As you can see, our first day of surveillance wasn't very productive. Mary Anne and I had been excited by our sighting of the green car, but once we calmed down we realized it didn't mean much. Later, though, I had an idea. I went to the library that night, took out some books, and studied them carefully. Then I called Kristy and asked her to join me and Mary Anne at the pet shop the next day. I had a feeling she might be helpful.

We met after school and headed into town on our bikes. All the other BSC members were teamed up again, but Mary Anne and Kristy and I were the only ones going to the pet shop. Jessi and Mal were planning to roam around on their bikes, watching for the green car, and Stacey and Claud were staking out the Tates'. (I think they were curious about that "rich and famous" lifestyle.)

Kristy led the way into town, taking a long route that covered a lot of streets we don't normally ride through. "We might as well watch for the green car," she explained. "It could be anywhere, anytime. There are dogs in every neighbourhood in Stoneybrook."

"How's David Michael doing?" I asked, as I huffed and puffed to keep up with her.

"Terrible," said Kristy. "He's not eating,

105

he's not sleeping very well, and he's falling behind in school because he can't concentrate. I'm worried about him."

"Poor David Michael," said Mary Anne. "I wonder . . . do—do you think he might want to borrow Tigger for a few days?"

Wow. Mary Anne is so sweet, and so sensitive. It would be a huge sacrifice for her to give up Tigger even for a few days. But she would do it, if it would make David Michael feel better.

"Thanks, Mary Anne," said Kristy. "But I don't really think it would help. Besides, Boo-Boo would probably terrorize Tigger." Boo-Boo is Watson's cat, and he's old and fat and bad-tempered.

Mary Anne looked relieved. But even so, she said, "Well, let me know if you change your mind."

By the time we reached the pet shop, the three of us were out of breath. We leaned against our bikes for a few minutes, resting. "When we go in," I said, "just follow my lead and let me do the talking. But listen and watch closely, okay?" Mary Anne and Kristy nodded. I led them into the shop. I walked up and down the aisles, and they followed behind me.

"Oh, isn't that a sweet little beagle?" I said, pointing to a puppy in the first cage we passed. "Remember, *beagle*," I whispered to them.

"Beagle," Mary Anne and Kristy whispered obediently.

The next cage held a fluffy white dog. "That's a Samoyed," I said. "When it grows up, it'll be big enough to pull a sledge, like a husky does." I turned and whispered again, "Samoyed." They nodded.

"Shar Pei," I said, pointing into the next cage. "That dog is Chinese."

"How do you know the names of all these dogs?" Kristy asked. She sounded impressed.

"I did some research," I replied, whispering. "I took these dog books out of the library. It was sort of fun."

Mary Anne was still looking at the Shar Pei, and now she giggled. "It's all wrinkly," she said. "It looks so soft."

"Just remember," I whispered. "Shar Pei." I meant business.

"Shar Pei," they whispered back.

We walked down the rows, looking into every cage. I told my friends the breed of every dog, and made sure they remembered the names. Then, when we'd looked them all over, I pulled them into a huddle. "Okay," I said. "They have a beagle, a Samoyed, a Shar Pei, a Rottweiler, an Airedale, and a Scottish terrier, right?" We nodded. "So let me think for a second," I said. "What *don't* they have?" After a second I snapped my fingers. "Got it," I said. "This is perfect." I walked quickly to the front of the shop, with Mary Anne and Kristy behind me. (I knew they were dying of curiosity, but I had to act fast now that I was ready.) I approached a salesman. "Do you have a Saint Bernard?" I asked.

"No," said the salesman, smiling. "I mean, not right at the moment. But we can probably get you one. It would be expensive, though. You'd have to pay several hundred dollars up front if you want a pedigree."

I nodded, trying to look thoughtful. "I'll have to ask my parents," I said to the man. "Thanks!" Then I led my friends out of the shop.

"Just as I suspected," I said, when we'd reached the pavement. "There's something strange about the way that shop works. Don't you think most salesmen would have recommended a breeder, or at least told us when certain dogs were due in. But he—"

"Hey!" Kristy said, interrupting me. "There goes the green car. Let's follow him!" The same man was driving: the owner of the shop. We jumped on our bikes and rode after him, but we couldn't keep up for long. While we were stuck in slow traffic it was easy, but once he turned off the main street of Stoneybrook, we lost him.

After my experiment, I felt that we were

coming close to working out the case. I had my suspicions, and we had more and more information to go on, but there was still no way to put it together as proof that the police would believe. I had a feeling that the pet shop wasn't getting its dogs the way most pet shops do, but I couldn't put the whole picture together. Still, I felt encouraged.

12th CHAPTER

Thursday

I guess if I had a dog, I'd be pretty worried too. I mean, the way dogs are disappearing these days, I would be awfully careful. But poor Charlotte is letting her fears get the better of her. It's a good thing my friends and I have talked about how to help kids deal with their fears. Because of that, I felt that I handled things with Charlotte pretty well. Still, I don't think she's going to rest easy until this case is solved.

Stacey was sitting for Charlotte that afternoon, and Charlotte was in a total panic. She's a clever kid, and she reads the newspaper every night. And lately, the *Stoneybrook News* has been full of stories about—you've guessed it—disappearing dogs.

When Stacey arrived at the Johanssens', Charlotte was sitting on the living room floor. Her little dog Carrot, a schnauzer, was lying next to her. Charlotte was looking through a pile of newspaper clippings she had cut out. "Look at these, Stacey," she said. "Isn't it awful?"

Stacey sat down next to Charlotte and began to flip through the clippings. She saw a story about a little boy whose puppy had been stolen, and one about a couple who had lost their prize-winning English sheepdog. She even saw a story about a woman whose German shepherd had been stolen; a German shepherd she had been training to be a guide dog for a blind person.

Not all of these dogs had disappeared from homes in Stoneybrook. The thieves were apparently roaming all over a wide area, covering several towns. Even so . . .

"I'm so scared!" said Charlotte. "I don't know what I'd do if they took Carrot. And if they see him, I just know they'll take him. He's a pedigree schnauzer! Plus, he's very clever. Want me to show you how he can say his prayers?"

Stacey smiled. "I've seen him do that," she said. We've all seen it, and the fact is that it's a very cute trick. When you tell Carrot to say his prayers, he puts his paws in your lap and lays his head on them. But Stacey didn't think the thieves were necessarily looking for performing dogs. "It's a great trick," said Stacey. "But I think Carrot will be safe, as long as you keep an eye on him."

"But that's just the problem!" wailed Charlotte. "I can't watch him every minute. I have to go to school. And today, I have to rehearse with the other cheerleaders at the Krashers' practice. When I'm not with him, the thieves could take him."

Stacey could see that Charlotte was seriously afraid, and she knew better than to treat a child's fear lightly. "Well, let's see," said Stacey. "How can we make sure Carrot is safe?"

"I don't know," said Charlotte. "Maybe I should take him with me to the practice."

Stacey thought for a minute. "That might work out," she said, thinking that she could dog-sit while Charlotte cheered.

"No!" said Charlotte. "It's no good. He'd be out in the open, where anybody could see him. And if we turned our backs for even a second, they might take him."

"Well, then," said Stacey, "I think we should leave him at home."

"All alone?" asked Charlotte, looking as if she were about to cry. "Poor Carrot would never be able to run away fast enough if somebody tried to grab him. Anyway, he thinks everyone is his friend. He would just walk off with the thieves."

Stacey had to admit that Carrot was friendly. At that moment, he was licking her hand and gazing up at her lovingly. His big brown eyes gave him a trusting and innocent look. She patted his nose. "Good boy, Carrot," she said. "Charlotte, I really think he'll be safe at home," she said. "We'll leave him inside."

Charlotte frowned. "I don't know," she said. "Maybe I should just skip that Krushers' practice."

"That's not a good idea," said Stacey. "For one thing, Haley and Vanessa need you. And for another, it doesn't really solve the problem. What are you going to do when you go to school? You have to get used to the idea that Carrot is safe here."

Charlotte reached over and hugged Carrot. "I'm just so scared," she said. "Carrot is my best friend."

"I know," said Stacey gently. "But you know what? I think if you look through these clippings carefully, you'll see that none of those dogs were stolen from a locked house. They were all taken from gardens, or from public parks. See?" She passed the clippings back to Charlotte.

Charlotte read through each of the stories. "You're right," she said. "I think—I think it'll be okay to leave him here. But let's make sure that nobody can get in to steal him, okay?"

"It's a deal," said Stacey. "Let's take him for a little walk up and down the street first, and then we'll get him settled before we leave."

Charlotte ran to find Carrot's lead. "I know," she said. "We can set up a burglar alarm by the front door, so if the thieves *do* try to get in, Carrot will hear them. That will give him a chance to hide."

Stacey nodded. She knew that Carrot would be unlikely to run *away* from a noise, since he was a dog and dogs love to investigate. But she didn't bring that up, since she also knew it was even more unlikely that anyone would break in. Also, she wanted Charlotte to feel secure and confident.

During their walk Charlotte talked non-stop, planning ways to burglar-proof the house, and when they went back inside, she got busy. First she piled empty tin cans (which she found in the recycling bin in the garage) near the front door. "That'll make a racket if anybody comes in," she said. Then she put a bucket of water by the back door, thinking that it would be knocked over if the door was opened, and the spilled water would "slow them down". (Stacey could only hope that Dr Johanssen didn't get home early!) After that, she took Carrot's brush and combed all his hair the wrong way.

Stacey was mystified. "Why are you doing that?" she asked. She knew Charlotte must have a reason, and she couldn't wait to hear it.

"So he doesn't look as handsome," said Charlotte. "So far, the thieves have only taken good-looking dogs." She was busy combing Carrot's beard back so that it had almost disappeared. "And without his beard, he doesn't look much like a pedigree schnauzer, so maybe the thieves won't be interested."

Carrot was starting to look very strange, and very unhappy. "I think that's enough," said Stacey, feeling she ought to put a stop to things.

"Okay," said Charlotte. "One last thing." She coaxed Carrot into the study, gave him a big hug, and closed the door on him. Then she wrapped masking tape all around the handle, to "lock" him in. "There," she said, dusting off her hands. "That should do it."

"I would think so," said Stacey. "Now let's get going. We're late already!" Charlotte grabbed the pom-poms, and they headed out of the door and down the street. Stacey took Charlotte's hand. "Hurry!" she said. They were almost running. Stacey was concentrating on getting Charlotte to the practice on time, but she was still being responsible, too. She checked carefully at each crossing to make sure no cars were coming.

And at one of those crossings, as she glanced down a side street, she saw it. The green car. Or at least, *a* green car. She told me later that she couldn't be absolutely positive. She was moving too fast to be sure. And some bushes were in the way. But it looked like the green car we'd been watching for, and it was parked at the side of the street. And she *thought* she saw the door open, and she *thought* she saw someone reach out and pull something into the car!

"It all happened so fast," she said to me, when she reached the playground. I was there watching the Krashers practise, since I was sitting for Matt and Haley again. Charlotte had run over to join Vanessa and Haley, so Stacey and I were alone. "It was almost as if I didn't realize what I was seeing until *after* we'd gone past that spot. But I think maybe I actually saw the thieves steal a dog!"

"Stacey, are you sure?" I asked. I couldn't believe what I was hearing. I'd been trying to crack this case for days, and now an actual dog-napping might be going on almost under my nose.

"No, I'm not sure," said Stacey. "It happened too fast."

"Can you watch Matt and Haley for a minute?" I asked. "I'm going to run back to that street and look around." I stood up.

"No!" said Stacey, pulling my arm. "It's too dangerous. That's why we've been working in teams, remember? You can't go alone."

I stamped my foot in frustration. "Come with me, then," I said, even though I knew she couldn't.

"I can't," she said. "I'm responsible for Charlotte. It wouldn't be fair to leave Kristy alone with all these kids, and Bart hasn't arrived yet."

I stamped my foot again. I knew I was acting like a two-year-old, but I was just so angry. I was just on the verge of solving the case. All of a sudden, things were clicking into place for me, and I was beginning to understand how the thieves were operating. "I think I know what's going on!" I said to Stacey. "But I just can't *prove* it yet."

Stacey looked at me sympathetically. "I know you want to solve this case," she said, "and I bet you will. We'll all help. But the only thing we can do now is watch and wait."

13th CHAPTER

"Wake up, Dawn! It's a beautiful day, and we're going to a ball game!" Mary Anne was shaking my shoulder. I mumbled sleepily and tried to hide under the covers.

It was Saturday, the day of the big Krashers game in New Hope. Mary Anne was psyched up for the game, and I have to admit that I was quite excited, too. We knew the game was incredibly important to Kristy, and to all the kids on the team.

I tumbled out of bed and pulled on my jeans. "What time are we supposed to be at the Pikes'?" I asked.

"I told them we'd be there by ten, so we'd better get going fairly soon," said Mary Anne. "You have time for breakfast, though. Dad made pancakes!"

"Yum!" I said. *That* got me moving. I ate quickly, and soon we were on our way to the

Pikes'. Every single member of the Pike family was going to the game, which meant they'd be taking two cars. (The Pikes are used to travelling in a convoy like that.)

"You know what?" I said to Mary Anne, as we walked across our garden. "I've just decided something. I'm going to take a day off from the dog mystery, and really enjoy myself. I'm not going to think about it at all today."

"Great idea," said Mary Anne. "You deserve a day off from the case. Let's just have fun today."

We walked up to the Pikes' door and rang the bell.

"Mary Anne and Dawn are here!" shrieked Claire from inside, after she'd peeped through the window. "Can I let them in?"

"Sure!" I heard Mallory say.

Claire opened the door. "Hi, you silly-billy-goo-goos," she said. "How are you this silly-billy morning?"

"I'm silly-billy fine," I said.

"I'm goo-goo fine," said Mary Anne.

Claire fell down on the floor, laughing. It's so easy to make kids laugh.

"Hi, you lot," said Mal. "Ready to go? We are—almost."

Then we heard a shout from upstairs. "Where's my lucky penny?" yelled Nicky. "I can't play first base without my lucky penny!"

"Jordan stole it," called Adam, from the dining room.

"No, Byron has it," yelled Jordan, from the kitchen.

"Adam spent it on chewing gum," said Byron, running down the stairs.

"Adam!" Nicky wailed.

"No, I didn't," said Adam. "It's in your trainer. I saw it there yesterday."

"Phew," said Nicky. By that time he'd come downstairs, and he was rummaging in the cupboard. He was dressed in his Krushers T-shirt, since the kids had decided to wear their team shirts. "Okay," he said to himself. "Lucky penny. Glove. Hat. Clean socks. I guess I'm ready!"

"Me, too," said Vanessa, walking into the corridor. "It's a perfect day for a game of baseball, with leaves on the trees and birds and all!"

Good old Vanessa, the Poet of Slate Street. She was wearing her cheerleading outfit: a Krushers T-shirt, a flared denim skirt, white knee socks, and trainers. And she was carrying a banner that said, "GO KRASHERS! STONEYBROOK'S ALL-STARS."

Margo ran in behind Vanessa. "Uh-oh," muttered Mary Anne, nudging me. I looked at Margo's face and saw a familiar pout. It looked like the one Claire had been wearing ever since Kristy and Bart had announced the Krashers team line-up.

"Do we *have* to go?" asked Claire. "I don't want to see that stupid old game."

"Neither do I," said Margo, after a second. But she didn't sound so sure.

"You'll be sorry if you don't go," said Mallory. "It'll be fun. Anyway, there's nobody to look after you here at home, so you have to come along. Anyhow, you're supposed to help Kristy with the equipment, remember?"

Claire pouted even harder. "All right," she said. "We'll go. But we're *not* going to have fun." She folded her arms over her chest. "So there."

"So there," Margo echoed.

"Okay, everybody," said Mr Pike, dashing into the hall. "Time to get a move on. Let's load 'em up and move 'em out!" He and Mrs Pike herded everyone out the door and into the two estate cars. I climbed into the first one, along with Margo, Claire, and the triplets. Nicky, Vanessa, Mallory, and Mary Anne piled into the other one, which Mrs Pike was driving. Mr Pike pulled out of the driveway, and the other car followed.

"Here we go!" sang Claire. "On our way to the silly-billy ball game!"

"Where's the you-know-what?" asked Jordan, after we'd been driving for a minute.

"The what?" asked Adam.

"The S.B."

"Oh, the Sick Bucket?" asked Byron. "It's in the other car."

"Oh, no!" said Adam. "And Margo's in *this* car."

I suddenly remembered that Margo has a habit of getting carsick—and she was sitting right next to me. I turned to look at her. She looked fine, not green at all.

"I'm not going to be sick," she said. "I feel fine. I'm only sick on long trips."

"Well, *I'm* not sitting next to her," said Jordan. "Pull over, Dad. I want to swap places with Claire."

"Everybody stays where they are," said Mr Pike. "It's only a short trip. Margo, you speak up if you feel like you're going to—"

"Dad?" Margo said in a small voice. "I think I—"

"What? What?" asked Mr Pike, sounding frantic. He started looking in the rearview mirror, as if he were trying to work out whether he could pull over.

"I think I forgot my sweater," finished Margo.

"Oh," said Mr Pike, sounding relieved. "Well, that's okay. It's a nice warm day."

I was relieved too, but I kept a close eye on Margo during the rest of the trip, just in case. So did the triplets, whenever they took a break from singing silly songs about the Addams family. Claire was busy sticking her tongue out at Nicky whenever the other estate car was in view. Luckily, it really *is* a short trip to New Hope. Mr Pike followed the directions we'd been given, and found the park where the playing field was. We reached it without any illness or other disasters, and piled out of both cars.

Most of the other Krashers were already there, and Nicky ran to join them. Vanessa found Haley and Charlotte, and they started to practise their cheers. Mr and Mrs Pike took the other kids over to the benches, and Mary Anne and Mal and I went to say hello to Kristy.

She was looking nervous. "Hi, you lot," she said. "I was beginning to think you weren't going to make it."

"We're only five minutes late," said Mal. "That's a record for my family." She smiled, hoping Kristy would smile back, but Kristy was too nervous.

"The kids look great," commented Mary Anne. "It's going to be a fun game, no matter what."

"I think so too," said Bart, who had joined us. "But Kristy can't relax."

"I'll relax when it's over," said Kristy. "Right now I'm busy worrying about whether Nicky will remember how to make a double play, and whether Jackie will break any bones, and—"

"It'll be okay," I said. "Everybody's going to do their best. Have fun, Kristy— it's only a game, remember?" She gave me a weak smile, and I smiled back, giving her the thumbs-up sign. I looked at Mary Anne and Mal. "Let's go and find some seats," I said.

We wished Kristy and Bart good luck, and then walked through the crowd that was gathering. "Wow," said Mal. "There really are a lot of people here."

"Look!" said Mary Anne. "Hot dogs!" We saw a hot dog vendor, a bagel man, and a lemonade stand run by the brothers and sisters of kids on the New Hope team. I felt as if we were at a carnival or something. Mary Anne bought a hot dog and I bought a bagel. Then we each bought a cup of lemonade, and found seats on the benches. I saw Mrs Braddock opposite, and gave her a wave. Mr Rodowsky, Jackie's dad, was there too. This was really a big event.

Suddenly, a big cheer went up as the New Hope team ran out onto the field. "Wow, they look serious," I said. The kids were wearing full uniforms, and some of them looked fairly old. "This could be a tough—" I began, but just then the Krashers came out on to the field, led by Kristy and Bart. I jumped up and yelled, "Go, Krashers!"

There were fewer people to cheer for our team, but the Krashers still got a pretty big round of applause. Jackie Rodowsky swept off his cap and took a bow, and everybody laughed.

The team captains shook hands all around, and then the game began. The Krashers were up first. I saw Kristy give Matt Braddock a quick hug before he picked up a bat and approached home plate. He looked scared, but he gave a few practice swings that looked very professional. The New Hope pitcher, a kid with red hair and freckles, went into his windup. He threw the ball—hard!—and Matt swung.

"Strike one!" shouted the umpire.

"Wait for your pitch, Matt," called Kristy, signing at the same time. "Look 'em over." She pointed to her own eyes when she said that.

Matt got ready for the next pitch, and when it came he swung again. This time he connected.

"A double!" I yelled, standing up to see better. "All right, Matt!" Matt couldn't hear the cheers of the Stoneybrook fans, but he grinned at the crowd and raised his fist in the air.

From that point on, the game was really exciting. One of Bart's kids—the one named Jerry, I think—got a home run in the second innings, and then the New Hope team tied it up with a bunch of smaller hits.

Mary Anne and Mallory and I were screaming and giving each other the high five every time the Krashers made a good play. I could see Kristy on the sidelines, pacing up and down. She looked less nervous, and more excited. The teams were turning out to be a good match, and the Krashers looked as if they had a chance to win, if they played well.

It was in the seventh innings that I turned for a moment to look at the crowd and saw something out of the corner of my eye. A woman in a red jogging suit was passing through the park, walking a big brown dog. "Hey!" I said. For a second I was so surprised that I couldn't even catch my breath.

Mary Anne turned to follow my gaze. "What?" she asked. "Do you know her?"

"No," I said. "But I know her dog. That's Cheryl."

14th CHAPTER

I jumped to my feet. "Hey!" I said again.

"Hey!" echoed someone behind me. "You spilled my popcorn." I turned around and saw an angry-looking man holding an empty popcorn box. Popcorn was scattered all over his lap.

"I'm sorry," I said, "but I just saw—"

"Sit down in front," called someone else. "We can't see the game!"

I bent down quickly, knocking into the woman in the next seat.

"My drink!" she cried. A wet stain was spreading over her skirt.

"Sorry, sorry, sorry," I said, grabbing a paper napkin from Mary Anne and handing it to the woman. "Mary Anne!" I hissed. "Come on!" I grabbed her arm and pulled her after me.

"Excuse us, excuse us," said Mary Anne, as we stumbled along the row.

"Sorry!" I said, as I stood on someone's toe.

When we had finally made our way out of the stands and were on solid ground, Mary Anne pulled her arm away. "Dawn, are you crazy?" she asked. "Even if that *was* Cheryl, which seems doubtful, what are we going to do about it?"

"First of all," I said. "It was Cheryl. I'm sure of it. And you'll be sure, too, as soon as we find that woman and you can see the dog closer up. And second, when we *do* find them, we'll—we'll—oh, I don't know. We'll work that out when the time comes. Now let's go!" I started towards the little stream that tumbled along the edge of the park. That was where the woman and her dog had been heading. Mary Anne followed, reluctantly.

"Can you see her?" I asked. I was a little out of breath, partly just from the excitement.

"Nope," said Mary Anne. "She's nowhere in sight. And with that red suit on, we'd see her if she was. I think we've lost her."

"No chance," I said. "We *have* to find her. Let's keep looking." I jogged away from the stream and over towards a football field that lay on the other side of the park.

"Look!" said Mary Anne. "Is that her?" She pointed towards the car park.

I saw a flash of red. "It must be!" I said, breaking into a run. We ran as fast as we could towards the person in red. "Oh, no," I said, once we were close enough to see better. The person in red was a man. A park employee, in a red uniform. He was picking up litter from the car park. I bent over to catch my breath. I was so disappointed.

The man looked at Mary Anne and me. "Are you girls all right?" he asked.

"We're looking for a lady in a red jogging suit," I said, panting. "Did you see her go by?"

"She has a big brown dog with her," added Mary Anne, who was breathing hard, too.

"Haven't seen her," said the man. "Try the meadow, over there," he added, pointing. "Lots of people play with their dogs in the meadow."

"I can't see any meadow," I said. "Where is it?"

"Through the trees, there," he said. "You take that little path."

I looked at Mary Anne. "Should we try it?" I asked. I felt as if we were on a wild-goose chase. Or a wild-dog chase, in this case.

"We've come this far," she said. "We might as well." She smiled at me.

"All *right*!" I said, feeling determined

again. "Let's go." I thanked the man in red, and then we started out again. We cut through the woods and came out on the other side at the edge of a wide meadow. Dotted all over it were people and dogs. "He was right," I said. "There are a lot of dogs here. But is Cheryl one of them?" I scanned the area for any signs of red.

"I can see her!" said Mary Anne. "Over there!" She pointed, and I saw the woman standing on a little hill. She was throwing a frisbee for her dog. For Cheryl.

"That's her," I said. "It really is. Come on!" We jogged along. Soon we were close enough to get a really good look.

"That *is* Cheryl," said Mary Anne. "You were right. I know it's her because I remember that darker brown spot on her shoulder. It looks like a heart."

We stood and watched for a few seconds as the woman threw the frisbee and Cheryl ran to fetch it. "Good girl, Cleo," said the woman, when the dog returned with the Frisbee. "Good girl."

"Cleo?" I said under my breath. "Maybe her new name is Cleopatra." I was in a daze as I stood there watching Cheryl run and jump.

"What do we do now?" asked Mary Anne.

"Do?" I said. I hadn't worked that part

out yet. Should we confront the woman? Should we steal Cheryl back? We had to take *some* kind of action, but I couldn't decide what it should be. "Um," I said.

"Let's call the police," Mary Anne said. "I mean, you've been looking for some kind of real evidence, and here it is."

"You're right," I replied. "We've got to call them. They can't ignore *this*." Then I realized that we were standing in the middle of a big park. "But where's a phone?"

"Back by the car park!" said Mary Anne. "I bet there's one in that little building."

"Right," I said. "Okay, look. You stay here and keep an eye on the woman and Cheryl. If they try to leave, stall them. Keep them here until I get back."

Mary Anne looked desperate. "Stall them? How?"

"I don't know," I said. "Ask her some questions about her dog. People love to talk about their pets."

"Okay," said Mary Anne. "But hurry."

I took off running, back towards the path through the woods. My heart was beating fast, and my breath was uneven. When I reached the path, I slowed down because it was a little darker in the woods and I couldn't see as well. Even so, I tripped over a root and fell—hard. I lay sprawled on the ground for a second, and then made myself get up and keep jogging.

When I came out by the car park, I saw the man in red, still picking up litter. "Is there a phone somewhere?" I asked.

He looked at me. "There's one in there," he said, pointing towards the building. "Are you *sure* you're all right?"

I looked down at myself. My shirt was streaked with dirt and I had ripped the knee of my jeans. I pushed my hair back and felt twigs in it. "I'm okay," I said. "But I need to make a phone call." I ran to the building, hurried inside, and found the phone. My hands were shaking as I put in some change and dialled the police. "Good thing I remember that number," I said to myself.

"Stoneybrook Police," said the man who answered.

"This is Dawn Schafer," I said. "I'm calling from the park in New Hope. It's about the dog-theft case."

"Yes?" the man said, sounding a little impatient.

"There's a woman here with a dog that I happen to know was stolen last week."

"Maybe it's the dog's owner," said the policeman. "Maybe the dog has been found and returned."

"It's not," I said. "I know the owner.

This is a different woman. But she's got the stolen dog."

"Okay, listen," the officer said, a little wearily. "I'll put a call through to the New Hope sergeant, and he'll send someone out to check on it. Where exactly is the dog, and where are you right now?"

I told him, and he said to wait in the car park until the police arrived. "How long will they take?" I asked.

"A few minutes," he said. "Just be patient."

I ran back outside and paced around the car park. The man in red had gone by then, so there was nobody to talk to. I walked back and forth, back and forth, checking my watch every thirty seconds. I kept thinking of poor Mary Anne, waiting over in the meadow. I hoped for her sake that the woman was still playing with Cheryl. Stalling her wouldn't be easy.

Finally, after almost ten minutes, a police car pulled up and a smiling policewoman stepped out. "Are you the girl that phoned about the dog?" she asked.

"Yes," I said eagerly. "Come on!" I started to jog back towards the woods.

"Whoa, take it easy," said the policewoman. "I have to call in first and let headquarters know what I'm up to." She made a quick call on her radio, and then followed me through the woods and out into the meadow.

Mary Anne was standing near the spot where I'd left her. The woman was nearby, talking to another dog owner. Cheryl was playing with a black Labrador retriever. "Boy, am I glad to see you," Mary Anne said. "So far I haven't had to stall her, but I was sure she was going to decide to leave any minute."

"Which dog is it?" asked the policewoman.

"The brown one," I said.

She looked at Cheryl for a moment. "We do have a report on a missing Great Dane," she said. "Okay, let me do the talking here. Which woman was walking the dog?"

I pointed her out. The policewoman started across the meadow, and Mary Anne and I followed behind. "Excuse me, ma'am," said the officer. "New Hope police." She flashed her badge. "I just have a few questions about your dog."

"Cleo?" asked the woman. "What about her?"

"How long have you owned her?"

"About a week," said the woman. "I got her through a pet shop in Stoneybrook. I'd asked for a Great Dane weeks ago, and they finally got one in. She cost the earth, but she's worth it. Aren't you Cleo?" She smiled down at the dog. Then she looked back at the policewoman with a worried expression. "Is there a problem?" she asked.

"Yes!" I blurted out. "That dog was *stolen*! That's how that pet shop gets dogs. When you tell them what you want, they go out and steal it from someone else!" I was too excited to keep my mouth shut. Suddenly I knew that I'd been right about how the dog-theft ring operated. I still didn't know how or why Mr Tate was involved, but I was sure he was.

The woman looked shocked. "Stolen?" she asked. "But—but that's awful. If this is all true, someone must miss this dog very much!"

"They do," I said, thinking of the Mancusis.

"Can I ask you to come down to the station?" asked the policewoman. "Bring the dog along, and any receipts or papers you have for her. It looks as if we may be about to solve this case, thanks to these girls."

I smiled. Finally, somebody believed me.

"Hey, what's that noise?" asked Mary Anne. A roar had gone up from the direction of the baseball diamond. "I bet the game's over. Let's go and see who won."

The policewoman said she'd be in touch, and thanked us again. We took off running. We ran back through the woods, past the car park, and along the stream. And when we arrived at the baseball field, we could see

136

right away what had happened. There stood Bart and Kristy, surrounded by a crowd of very happy kids. "Hip, hip, hurray!" yelled the kids, tossing their hats in the air.

The Krashers had won the game.

15th CHAPTER

We ran to Kristy. "Kristy!" said Mary Anne. "You did it! You won!"

"We *did* it," said Kristy, looking dazed. "We actually won!"

Bart squeezed her shoulder. "How about that?" he said. "The Stoneybrook All-Stars really did it."

Mary Anne and I quickly told Kristy what had happened while she was busy coaching. She grinned. "Maybe they'll find Shannon now," she said. "But I'm not going to tell David Michael anything yet. I don't want to get his hopes up until we're sure."

The Krashers were milling around giving each other the high five and talking excitedly about the ninth innings' double play that Nicky and David Michael had made. Meanwhile, the New Hope team were looking dejected as they picked up their equipment and got ready to leave.

"Hey, you lot," said Kristy to the Krashers. "I think we forgot something. How about a cheer for the other team?" The kids stopped fooling around immediately, and gathered around Kristy and Bart.

"Two, four, six, eight, who do we appreciate!" they chanted. "New Hope! New Hope! Yeah!"

The cheer didn't seem to make the New Hope kids feel much better, but it was a nice gesture. Afterwards, the teams lined up and walked past each other, each kid shaking every other kid's hand as they passed. "Good game," they said to each other. "Nice pitching. Good game. Nice hitting."

Kristy couldn't stop grinning. "I still can't believe it," she said. "I never saw my kids play so well."

By then, most of the Stoneybrook fans were on the field. Mothers were hugging their kids, dads were giving the high five, and little sisters and brothers were dancing around happily. Even Claire and Margo were smiling, as if they'd finally forgotten the hurt of not being included.

"Hey, Mary Anne," I said, pulling her aside. "Will you come to the police station with me when we get back? I want to find out what happened with Cheryl and everything."

"Okay," she replied. "I expect Mr Pike will drop us off there on the way home."

Soon the Pikes were ready to leave. Mary Anne and I congratulated Kristy and Bart one more time. "We'll talk to you later," I said to Kristy. "As soon as we find out what's going on."

Mr Pike was glad to drop us off at the police station. "Sounds like you girls really helped to crack this case," he said. "I'm impressed!" Claire and Margo were impressed, too.

"Can I have your autographs?" asked Margo. She'd been collecting autographs from the Krashers, too.

"Of course," I said. "Don't lose this, now," I joked. "It may be valuable some day." I wrote my name on the scrap of paper she held out. So did Mary Anne. It was fun to feel like a hero.

The first thing we heard when we walked into that police station was barking. It sounded as if fifty dogs were in there! But we couldn't see them. They must have been in a back room.

"Hi!" I said to the policeman at the desk. He was the one I'd talked to twice before.

"Hi," he said. Then he looked at me more closely. "Oh, *hi*!" he repeated, sounding much more enthusiastic. "Hey, you were right about that car, and about Mr Tate and all. You're a really good detective, you know that?"

I blushed, but I was pleased. Now he couldn't treat me like a pest any more. "It was nothing," I said. "I just had a feeling, that's all. And I acted on it."

"Well, you did the right thing," he said. "That Tate character—" He was interrupted by loud barking.

"Is Cheryl here?" I asked.

"Is that the Great Dane?" he said. "She's here. So are a few of her doggie pals."

Just then a door flew open behind him, and Cheryl galloped out. A startled policeman came running behind her, and behind *him* was—

"Shannon!" said Mary Anne. She opened her arms, and Shannon ran to her. I saw Mary Anne's eyes fill with tears as she hugged Shannon and kissed her nose. "Oh, wow," she said. "Are Kristy and David Michael going to be glad to see you!"

"We've already notified her owners," said the policeman.

I bent down to pat her, too. "Good girl, Shannon," I said, feeling my own eyes begin to sting. "Were you scared? Everything's okay now. Kristy and David Michael will be here soon to take you home."

"Oh, Cheryl," I heard a voice behind me,

and I turned to see Mrs Mancusi bury her face in Cheryl's neck. Cheryl was wagging her tail as hard as she could, and trying to lick Mrs Mancusi all over. I felt a couple of tears spill down my cheeks as I watched their reunion. I was starting to understand the love that people have for their pets.

A couple of other dogs were running around; I recognized a Weimaraner and a little Pomeranian and pointed them out to Mary Anne.

"You really learned a lot about dogs, didn't you?" she said.

I grinned. "All that studying."

Just then, Mrs Mancusi stood up and smiled at the police officer. "How can I thank you?" she said. "I'm so happy to have my baby back."

Cheryl didn't look like much of a baby to me, except maybe a baby *horse*.

"Don't thank me," said the policeman. "Thank that girl over there, and her friends. They're the ones who solved the case."

Mrs Mancusi turned and noticed us for the first time. "Dawn!" she exclaimed. "Mary Anne. Did you girls have something to do with this?"

I didn't know what to say.

"They certainly did," said the policeman. "They tracked down the number plate of the vehicle involved in the thefts. They also spotted your dog over in New Hope and called us in to check out the situation."

"That's incredible," said Mrs Mancusi. "You must have been working really hard on this."

"Well, I felt responsible for Cheryl's being stolen," I mumbled.

"Oh, Dawn," said Mrs Mancusi. "It wasn't your fault. We never thought that."

"I know," I said. "Still, I wanted to do whatever I could to get her back."

"Well, I really am glad you did," she replied. "Cheryl says she is, too. Right, Cheryl?" Cheryl cocked her ears and wagged her tail and—I swear this is true—she smiled. "But who stole the dogs—and why?" Mrs Mancusi asked the policeman.

"Karl Tate stole them," said the policeman.

"Karl Tate?" repeated Mrs Mancusi. "But he's one of the richest men in Stoneybrook."

"Not any more," said the policeman. "Apparently he's been losing a bundle in the property market. So he came up with some schemes for making money and offered them around. The pet shop people were the first ones to bite. What they did was steal dogs—to order. They'd get a customer who was looking for a Great Dane, you see, and then the next thing you know—"

"Cheryl gets stolen," finished Mrs Mancusi. "What kind of people would steal dogs from their owners?" she went on, shaking her head. "What a horrible thing to do."

"Lucrative, though," said the policeman. "They found out there was big money in it. In fact, there was more money in stealing dogs than in running a pet shop. A lot of the time they didn't even bother to open the shop."

Mary Anne looked at me, eyebrows raised. "That's why it wasn't open that day I cycled into town," she whispered to me.

"Anyway," the policeman went on, "they're all under arrest now, Mr Tate and the couple who owned the shop. I don't think any more dogs are going to be stolen around *here*!" He grinned at me, and I grinned back.

"Have you found *all* the dogs that were stolen?" I asked.

"Not quite. There were a few out at Tate's house," said the policeman. "This one here," he pointed to Shannon, "and those other two. We're tracking down the rest of them—the ones that were already sold. Everybody should have their dogs back within a few days."

"Shannon!" I heard Kristy shout, behind me. She had just run in, along with David Michael. They both knelt on the floor, and Shannon jumped all over them, squirming and wriggling with joy. David Michael looked even happier than he had when the Krashers won their game.

"Hi, you lot," said Kristy, when she finally stood up. "There was a message at home for us to come down here. I can't believe Shannon's safe and sound! Isn't this great?"

We nodded, smiling. David Michael and Shannon were still rolling around on the floor.

"Are you girls ready to have your pictures taken?" asked the police officer.

"What?" I said.

"The *Stoneybrook News* called a little while ago. They want to interview you, and put your pictures in the paper. They'll be here any minute." He smiled. "You can use the ladies' room to clean up, if you want."

I remembered the twigs in my hair and the mud on my shirt. "Thanks," I said. Then I turned to Kristy and Mary Anne. "While I clean up, can you lot call everybody?" I asked. "I want every member of the BSC to be in this picture, since you all helped."

It was fun being interviewed, and the photographer let us pose any way we wanted to. Our picture was going to look really cool. But it was a relief when the photographers left and it was just us—the good old BSC—again.

We trooped out of the police station and went to the coffee shop, where Bart and Logan were waiting to meet us. It was time for a celebration! We laughed and talked and discussed every detail of the case we'd solved and the game the Krashers had won. But after a while, I grew quiet, thinking about what I'd learned about people and their pets. And when we left the coffee shop, I took Mary Anne aside for a second.

"Want to stop by the pet shop?" I asked. "The old one, I mean."

"Okay," she said. "But why do *you* want to go there?"

"To buy a treat for Tigger," I told her. "And then we'll go home and give it to him—and I might even let him kiss me!"

Look out for Mystery No 8

JESSI AND THE JEWEL THIEVES

Without a word to each other, Quint and I simultaneously slouched down in our seats so that we couldn't be seen from the window. But there was no way we were about to stop listening.

The argument seemed to be gathering steam. "I've had it with you," said Frank. "You may be an expert on jewels, but that's not enough. I need a partner who isn't going to wimp out on me."

"Just give me some time, Frank," said Red. "These aren't just any jewels we're talking about, you know. The cops are going to go wild when this stuff turns up missing."

Jewels! This was getting better and better.

"I keep telling you," said Frank, "we don't need to worry about the cops. We'll be long gone before they even know the jewels are missing."

"I don't know," said Red again, looking

stubborn. "Let's go over the plan one more time."

"*No!*" yelled Frank. "We've been over it a million times. You're either with me or *not* with me. And I gotta tell you, if you back out now, I'll kill you!"

Quint grabbed my arm, and I grabbed his. This was getting serious. I had no doubt that Frank meant what he said. He looked really capable of killing somebody. He was tough and mean-looking, and if I were Red I would be running out of the room.

Just then, Quint's father opened the door to the TV room. "Quint! Jessi!" he called "Turn down that TV! Morgan and Tyler are trying to get to sleep."

Quint and I looked at each other. My first impulse was to giggle. This was a real fight we were listening to, not the TV. We couldn't turn it down if we wanted to. But then I saw the panicked look in Quint's eyes, and I realized that this was no laughing matter. Quint's dad had just yelled out our names, loud enough for Frank and Red to hear. I turned to look out of the window, and saw that the two of them had stopped arguing. Instead, they were staring across at us!

The Babysitters Club

Need a babysitter? Then call the Babysitters Club. Kristy Thomas and her friends are all experienced sitters. They can tackle any job from rampaging toddlers to a pandemonium of pets. To find out all about them, read on!

GREEN WATCH by Anthony Masters

BATTLE FOR THE BADGERS

Tim's been sent to stay with his weird Uncle Seb and his two kids, Flower and Brian, who run Green Watch – an environmental pressure group. At first Tim thinks they're a bunch of cranks – but soon he finds himself battling to save badgers from extermination . . .

SAD SONG OF THE WHALE

Tim leaps at the chance to join Green Watch on an anti-whaling expedition. But soon, he and the other members of Green Watch, find themselves shipwrecked and fighting for their lives . . .

DOLPHIN'S REVENGE

The members of Green Watch are convinced that Sam Jefferson is mistreating his dolphins – but how can they prove it? Not only that, but they must save Loner, a wild dolphin, from captivity . . .

MONSTERS ON THE BEACH

The Green Watch team is called to investigate a suspected radiation leak. Teddy McCormack claims to have seen mutated crabs and sea-plants, but there's no proof, and Green Watch don't know whether he's crazy or there's been a cover-up . . .

GORILLA MOUNTAIN

Tim, Brian and Flower fly to Africa to meet the Bests, who are protecting gorillas from poachers. But they are ambushed and Alison Best is kidnapped. It is up to them to rescue her *and* save the gorillas . . .

SPIRIT OF THE CONDOR

Green Watch has gone to California on a surfing holiday – but not for long! Someone is trying to kill the Californian Condor, the bird cherished by an Indian tribe – the Daiku – and without which the tribe will die. Green Watch must struggle to save both the Condor and the Daiku . . .

THE UNDERWORLD TRILOGY
Peter Beere

When life became impossible for the homeless of London many left the streets to live beneath the earth. They made their homes in the corridors and caves of the Underground. They gave their home a name. They called it UNDERWORLD.

UNDERWORLD

It was hard for Sarah to remember how long she'd been down there, but it sometimes seemed like forever. It was hard to remember a life on the outside. It was hard to remember the real world. Now it seemed that there was nothing but creeping on through the darkness, there was nothing but whispering and secrecy.

And in the darkness lay a man who was waiting to kill her . . .

UNDERWORLD II

"Tracey," she called quietly. No one answered. There was only the dark threatening void which forms Underworld. It's a place people can get lost in, people can disappear in. It's not a place for young girls whose big sisters have deserted them. Mandy didn't know what to do. She didn't know what had swept her sister and her friends from Underworld. All she knew was that Tracey had gone off and left her on her own.

UNDERWORLD III

Whose idea was it? Emma didn't know and now it didn't matter anyway. It was probably Adam who had said, "Let's go down and look round the Underground." It was something to tell their friends about, something new to try. To boast that they had been inside the secret Underworld, a place no one talked about, but everyone knew was there.

It had all seemed like a great adventure, until they found the gun . . .

Also by Peter Beere

CROSSFIRE

When Maggie runs away from Ireland, she finds herself roaming the streets of London destitute and alone. But Maggie has more to fear then the life of a runaway. Her step-father is an important member of the IRA – and if he doesn't find her before his enemies do, Maggie might just find herself caught up in the crossfire . . .

HIPPO ANIMAL STORIES

*If you like animals, then you'll love
Hippo Animal Stories!*

Look out for:

Animal Rescue by Bette Paul

Tessa finds life in the country *so* different from life in
the town. Will she ever be accepted? But everything
changes when she meets Nora and Ned who run the
village animal sanctuary, and becomes involved in a
struggle to save the badgers of Delves Wood
from destruction . . .

Thunderfoot by Deborah van der Beek

Mel Whitby has always loved horses, and when she
comes across an enormous but neglected horse in a
railway field, she desperately wants to take care of it.
But little does she know that taking care of
Thunderfoot will change her life forever . . .

A Foxcub Named Freedom
by Brenda Jobling

A vixen lies seriously injured in the undergrowth. Her
young son comes to her for comfort and warmth. The
cub wants to help his mother to safety, but it is
impossible. The vixen, sensing danger, nudges him
away, caring nothing for herself – only for
his freedom . . .